Look How Happy I'm Making You

STORIES

Polly Rosenwaike

DOUBLEDAY  NEW YORK

These stories first appeared, in slightly different form, in the following publications: "Grow Your Eyelashes," *Indiana Review,* Summer 2012; "Field Notes" (as "Laboratory on the Moon"), *WomenArts Quarterly Journal,* Summer 2013; "White Carnations," *Prairie Schooner,* Spring 2012, reprinted in *The O. Henry Prize Stories 2013;* "Tanglewood," *New England Review,* Fall 2014; "June," *Copper Nickel,* Fall 2015; "Ten Warning Signs of Postpartum Depression," *Glimmer Train,* Fall 2017; "Welcome to Your Family," *Colorado Review,* Spring 2016; "A Lady Who Takes Jokes," *Iron Horse Literary Review,* 2015; "Parental Fade," *New Delta Review,* December 2013.

Jacket painting: Joan (Walker 44), 1986 © *2018 Alex Katz/Licensed by VAGA at Artists Rights Society (ARS), NY.*
Photograph: Private Collection © *Christie's Images/Bridgeman Images*
Jacket design by Emily Mahon

LIBRARY OF CONGRESS CATALOGING-IN-PUBLICATION DATA
Names: Rosenwaike, Polly, author.
Title: Look how happy I'm making you : stories / Polly Rosenwaike.
Description: First edition. | New York : Doubleday, 2019.
Identifiers: LCCN 2018024224 | ISBN 9780385544030 (hardcover) |
ISBN 9780385544047 (ebook)
Subjects: LCSH: Pregnancy—Fiction. | Motherhood—Fiction |
Fertility, Human—Fiction.
Classification: LCC PS3618.O8437 A6 2019 | DDC 813/.6—dc23
LC record available at https://lccn.loc.gov/2018024224

For Cody

& because of you,

for Zia & Ani too

Contents

Look How Happy I'm Making You

Grow Your Eyelashes

We are all in love with the baby. We, meaning the #4 bus community, weekdays at the seven o'clock hour, on our way to work and school and early morning errands. The baby wears a royal blue puffy jacket and a striped knit hat. He tracks our shopworn, overly articulated faces. Despite how we caper—tilting and bouncing our heads, scrunching our lips and wriggling our noses, working our hands into frantic waves—the baby gazes at us with his grave baby face. He is chary with his baby gift of a grin, a palm in the air, a mimic, obliging just often enough to lend hope to our campaigns. The father is charming, an early-thirties smiler with warm eyes and skin. Perhaps South American, his soft voice generous with the vowels. Strapped to the father's chest, the baby flaps his arms. There is something of a bird in him, both cautious and confident. Something of a bird, and a sad little clown, and a medicine man, and all of the possibilities that are open to a baby. We look at him longer than we would look at anyone else we don't actually know—and he will not say, or even think, that it is rude to stare.

I say that we are all in love with the baby, but probably there is someone on this bus who is not. Probably someone looks out the window, or at the affable father, or at her own lap, and thinks, goddamn that baby. This person is not swayed by the miniature hands, the swollen cheeks, the exploratory chirps—not swayed by this new human, welcomed as if he belongs to all of our delicate hopes and magnanimous impulses. As other faces soften, she hardens hers. I am willing to believe that there is such a person in our cozy bus community, with the chatty women and the tenderly grizzled men, and the driver who says "So long, little guy" when the baby leaves, borne aloft by his father.

We are trying, my husband Kevin and I. If only that meant we were trying to teach a monkey to do sign language; or trying out this new robot that cleans bathrooms; or trying to save the world, one polar ice cap at a time. But when you are a childless couple in your mid-thirties with two full-time jobs and a three-bedroom house, everyone knows what trying means. Making love, we used to think penis or breasts, vagina or balls. Thought them hard, as the dependable pleasure things they were. Then we thought baby, almost sexier than sex for sex, a mystery beyond tit-for-tat physical love. We thought not quite sperm and egg, those clinical, unlovely words, but something like seed pearl embryo pregnant fetus heartbeat fingers toes belly bump love genius baby. We have been thinking this baby into limbo existence for eleven months now. The baby isn't coming. The baby is perched somewhere, her fist in her fierce, dainty mouth. I picture her the way Christian children are taught to think of babies God hasn't released from heaven yet. A peck of them fully formed and squeaky clean, enthroned in clouds, parents an unnecessary earthly contrivance.

K evin and I have the kind of grown-up jobs that cause people to nod politely when we say what we do and not ask any follow-up questions. I work as a web developer for a creative agency and Kevin's a software engineer. I wear my peasant blouses and flared skirts on the bus, and he drives to work in his suit. Though he could dress more casually, he likes the advantage the formality gives him. He's not especially handsome, but his shirt is crisp, his tie well chosen, his fingernails trimmed, and his hair nicely kept, neat with a bit of bounce. What more can a man do?

Before we met, I had hoped to find someone in an old-fashioned, romantic way: at a coffee shop, on a train, at my high school reunion (the guys I hoped to meet again were the ones I hadn't talked to in high school, whose sleepy, sexy faces I stared at through an algebra or social studies haze). At the fifteen-year reunion, I was cornered by Georgia, who, when tests were handed back in class, would immediately turn around and ask me what grade I got. She had become a middle school guidance counselor. She went on about "my kids," and how cute and troubled they were, while I eyed whatever men didn't seem to have a woman attached to them. The only one I talked to smelled like sardines and laughed when I said things that weren't at all funny.

After that I gave up and went online. At first the array of men was like the lure of the grocery store at midnight: shelves piled high with shiny goods, until you look closer and realize they're all filled with corn syrup. But Kevin didn't try to market himself with a glossy sheen. We skipped the coquettish emails and the hesitant phone calls and went right to sleeping together. He would undress in my living room—the wingtip shoes, the argyle socks, the creased pants, the boyish undershirt. His boxers were soft and worn. There was the thrill of a kind and decent naked man in my apartment. It happened slowly, first body and then mind, my skin leading the charge: love him, love him.

On the second date we established that both of us wanted kids, preferably two, but we weren't in a rush. And then suddenly, in the way that even the passage of three years can feel sudden, we were. Now, the more we wait, the more rushed we are. Every twenty-eight days, I mark an S in my pocket calendar, for old Aunt Sally. She is miserably punctual, though once it was thirty-two days. I couldn't get to sleep on night thirty-one. I kept squirming around in bed until Kevin caught me.

"Hey, tell me what's going on."

I didn't want to get his hopes up, but I couldn't help myself. "My period's late. Just by a few days, but."

"Yeah? How do you feel?"

"Fine. Anxious. Maybe a tiny bit nauseated."

Kevin circled my belly button with his finger. "Let's start music lessons early. Maybe at four?"

"Five might be better. Something cool. Viola. Or oboe."

"Oboe, are you crazy? Piano. Pianos don't squeak. Anyone can play the piano."

"Are you saying our kid would be just anyone?"

This kind of banter had been forbidden for months. We picked it up now like AAers playing a drinking game. We knew the risks, but we hoped that this time would be different.

My period came at work, in the bathroom, with its tastefully arranged display of tampons in a basket, as a courtesy to the female employees. I sat on the toilet and pictured babies living in the sewer system, playing in filth, but somehow still clean and happy, a gang of naked bottoms and fuzzy heads, throwing balls of shit and yelping with glee. When I got home, I had to tell Kevin, which I did by making sure the tampon wrapper was visible in the trash. We held on to each other for a while, and then we splintered off into our depressive habits: he read a million Amazon reviews for some dumb little thing we needed to buy, and I mapped out elaborate routes and accommodations for exotic trips we weren't going to take.

One Saturday I make the mistake of going to the mall. My sister's birthday is in a week, and I'd like to send her an interesting piece of clothing. Just inside the mall's entryway, I'm greeted by a woman on a sign. A beautiful woman, though not high-cheek-boned, sultry-lipped, stone-cold beautiful. The idea is, she's the kind of beautiful I might be if I tried harder and listened to the voices that are trying to help me. "Grow Your Eyelashes," this voice says. There is, apparently, a scientific formula for it. The eyelashes on the woman who could be me look noticeably mascara-laden, but they're not crazy long. Perhaps my doppelgänger is just about to call the phone number presented here. She knows her eyelashes are okay, but that they could be even better. She is on the verge of possessing the eyelashes she's always wanted, not falsies but real ones, cultivated from her very own eyelids.

Inside the mall I go from store to store, looking for something worthy of my sister Audrey, who has set up her stylish life just the way she wants it, in her mid-century modern house, with her husband Jeff and their two chickens. Patsy and Cline have a coop in the garden, where they take daily strolls through the sweet alyssum, nodding agreeably. When they want company, they press their beaks to the back door. You pick them up and stroke their feathers, and they expand to fill your arms. As a girl I tended to my dolls every day—otherwise they would miss me—and Audrey, two years my junior, could be conscripted to join, but she coddled no babies of her own. She played the movie-star aunt in a feather boa and plumed hat. "I'm back from Paris," she'd say. "Have an Eiffel Tower." An Eiffel Tower was anything she could stack up that wasn't blocks: Oreos, beanbags, packets of pocket tissues. I dressed the dolls and brushed their hair, and she let towers fall in their laps. She's an architect now, specializing in sustainable public projects, and she serves on several boards and has season tickets to the best local performing arts events.

"We don't feel the need for children," Audrey told our mother last Thanksgiving. "You have to need them, I think. So much that you don't think you can be happy without them."

Mom shook her head, proud and sad on its wrinkled neck. "That's not how it works. You can't know the joy until—" She swiped at a tear that was about to fall into the wild rice stuffing. "You just can't know it."

"Look how happy I'm making you," Audrey said.

The women's clothing departments are highlighting bizarre colors this season: salmon pink, pea green, recycle-bin blue, and styles that make no sense: three-quarter sleeves, capri pants, short-sleeved sweater dresses, T-shirts with collars. I don't have to look long in each store to decide—nope, nada. The salesladies ask if they can help, but how could they? Finally, in a Macy's daze, I get Audrey a cream-colored, cable-knit sweater. There is nothing offensive or unique about it. I'm tempted to buy one for myself too, but I don't want us to look like twins, even in two different states. If I had twins, I would give them names that sounded nothing like each other. Susannah and Mim, Theodore and Aziz. One twin would wear airplane pajamas; the other, stripes. I wouldn't call them the twins, nor would I perform experiments on them to see how alike they were. It would be very hard to have two babies, one on each breast, but with twins we'd have ourselves a family in one go. Two adults, two children, the sturdiness of four.

I call Audrey on her birthday, and when the phone connects, I hear the clinking around her before she says hello. She and Jeff are having brunch with friends.

"Go back to it," I tell her. "Eat your eggs Benedict."

"Yup, that's what I'm having," she says.

"And a bloody Mary?"

"Just OJ. Hey, thanks for the sweater. It's really cozy."

"I wanted to get you something with interest, as Mom would say, but there was nothing out there. The mall is a travesty."

"Did you hear me? I said I like it."

"Well, wear it in good health, as Grandma would say if she were alive."

"You sound depressed."

"Go back to your birthday brunch," I yell, as if volume equals enthusiasm, and end the call. When we lived near each other, Audrey would notice if I got a haircut, or new shoes, or new earrings. She would also tell me that I looked tired, or that my concealer wasn't concealing, or that my jeans had gone beyond fashionably worn. Now that we don't see each other much, she comments on the sound of my voice. I know she doesn't intend to be nosy or mean. She intends to be accurate. Over the years I've found her accuracy refreshing, intimate. Lately it makes me wish I had a quiet, oblivious brother.

O n the bus, the baby stares me down. Of course I am staring him down. I don't know which one of us started it. I'm standing across from him in complete winter garb, grasping the bar with a gloved hand. When I move to let an older woman take the one remaining seat, the baby turns his head to follow me. What attracts his attention at this stage in life, a matter of months? The deep red of my coat, the toggle buttons protruding from it, a feminine face probably about his mother's age? Despite the gold ring on the cute father's finger, I pretend that he's on his own, a single parent. Not knowing his name, I think of him as Javier. What happened to the woman who bore Javier's adorable child? She loves Uruguay more, with its rolling plains and ample rivers and her whole family there, all the aunts and cousins and children to care for as if they were her own. Or she is off with another one of her photojournalists, knowing the baby will fare better with his caring and dependable father. Or she died right after the birth, a complication no one could have foreseen or prevented. Yes, Javier seems too smiley to have endured the recent loss of his love, but it's his personality—wondrously compassionate and ever-hopeful—and now there's his son to think of too. Besides, everyone knows that only children smile out of sheer delight. In a real adult smile, there is always something other than happiness.

From our bus flirtation, Javier and I will fall in love. We'll conduct our affair gently, maturely, out of respect for Kevin (whom I still love, of course, but how can one

anticipate the sudden flowering of an even greater love?).
And out of respect for the baby, who has already suffered
the trauma of his mother's loss, if only in the unknowing
depths of his developing brain. Eventually I'll tell Kevin,
who will act all aggrieved, but who may already, behind his
disappointed eyes, be considering the possible benefits of
my betrayal. He could find someone prettier, more positive
and proactive. Someone younger, ridiculously fertile. After
the right amount of time has passed, we'll wish each other
well, and a second-chance peace will reign over our new
households. Javier's baby—and mine, yes mine now—will
become less bird, more human. He'll walk on his own, and
stamp his feet and scream. He'll patch words together
to make sentences that articulate his pleasures and his
sorrows.

But for now, I have spoken no words to Javier. The
chatty middle-aged women have all the small talk
covered. Occasionally one of the tenderly grizzled men
will wink at Javier, as if the noble state of fatherhood is an
acknowledgment between them.

I'm pregnant," Audrey says.
It's nine or so at night, and Kevin is in the next room,
scrolling through the *New York Times* by laptop light. I keep
quiet. Audrey had one abortion, four years ago, when she
and Jeff were recently married. She told me and only me,
certainly not our mother. She was relieved to be able
to exercise the right to not have a child long before it

would become a child, and she didn't seem to have ever regretted it.

"What do you think I should do?" Audrey asks now.

"What? I mean, what do you want?"

"I might have it. I wasn't planning to get pregnant, but maybe I'll just let it happen this time. Maybe Mom's right, and once I have a kid, I won't be able to imagine my life without it."

"What does Jeff think?"

"He's not thrilled, but he'll go along with it. He's not going to punch me in the stomach or push me down the stairs."

It occurs to me that she might have a miscarriage anyway, and I try to discard the thought.

"Now's the part where you're supposed to say I'd make a good mother."

"You would," I squeak. Audrey laughs.

"Who knows, right? You're the one who always liked babies. But hey, maybe we'll end up doing it together."

I offer no assent, no sisterly chuckle. I haven't told her, or anyone, that Kevin and I have been trying. Why discuss such things? Why say that you're attempting to grow out your eyelashes? Why not wait until they grow too long, stick out from your eyelids like a rooster's crown, sweep down your cheeks like a Chinese fan. If Audrey were around, I would ask her to trim them. Only she would have a steady enough hand, a careful enough eye. She would say, "You fool," and then fix me up. I would close my eyes and tilt back my head, hear the satisfying snip of scissors cutting through abundance. Could you make a wish on an apron full of eyelashes? Would their numbers strengthen the wish's power? Or is it only the chance falling of a single eyelash that makes it worth a wish?

Audrey chooses to ignore my silence, to spare me this time—or maybe she's too wrapped up in her own expanding life.

After we've ended the call, Kevin comes into the room and changes into his pajamas. "What's new with Audrey?" he asks, and when I tell him, since he'll find out sooner or later, he says, "Just like that, huh, by accident?"

"Sounds like it."

He settles heavily into bed, tugging the covers to his side. "Well I think we should stop trying to make it happen by accident."

"Yeah, I'm following the calendar. You know, sex isn't always a spontaneous seduction."

"I mean we've got to get some help. Do the tests, follow the steps. It's been long enough. Over a year."

"I know how long it's been."

"But you don't think we should do anything."

I do think we should do things. I could carry around three hazelnuts; he could carry a mandrake root. We could place a small statue of a fertility goddess beside our bed. We could make a pilgrimage to this hill in England with a chalk outline of a giant sporting an enormous erection. And when all of the magical rituals have failed, we can make an appointment at a fertility clinic like the other sensible and desperate childless couples.

"That's not true," I say, but Kevin is already after me, because he is a person who believes in taking practical action and does so, and I am a person who dreams about taking radical action and does nothing.

"So fine, it's easy for people like your sister who never even wanted a baby. Sometimes you have to work at things, give them a chance before you roll your eyes. What if you do become a mother? Are you going to teach our kid to give up, throw in the towel—it's just too hard?"

I thump out of bed, angry in my underwear. Kevin grazes my hand. "I'm sorry, I didn't mean it."

"No, go ahead. Be harsh."

I stand blinking in the doorway, watching him blink. It's one of those things you never think about until you do, and then how strange, the constant flickering of everyone's eyelids. But imagine a person who didn't blink, who stared at you with unshielded irises, like a picture in a biology book, like a doll, like the dead.

I didn't want to have to invest my faith and hope in medical technology. I wanted Audrey's surprise-surprise. To suddenly have a flower waterfall sea tendrils shooting stars flutter-kicking misty-eyed lullaby blooming through me. I wanted the romantic view of life to win out this time.

The baby and Javier—though that is surely not his name—haven't been on the bus for almost a month. The flu, I thought at first, in its heyday season. Then I envisioned a long vacation, the baby's first flight. But I am coming to believe in a more permanent, mundane reason for their disappearance. The dad goes to work at a different hour now. The baby attends another daycare. They have a new car, with the radio on, heat flowing from the vent, and the baby in a car seat, flapping his arms for no one to see.

The chatty people on the bus confer with each other over weariness and weather. Spring is on its way, they agree. Yup, winter is out like a bad dream. The bus driver says, "So long, big guy," to the kid who seems barely old enough to ride the bus alone, with his Batman backpack and his Spiderman shoes kicking the air above the floor. My mom calls to crow about Audrey's pregnancy; to plan a baby shower; to assure me it's okay that Audrey's going to have a baby first even though she's the younger sister, because my turn will come, she just knows it. Audrey tells me that she is throwing up, she is showing, she is considering cloth diapers, she is priming the chickens for the arrival of their human sibling. I let them do the talking; I ask the solicitous questions a loving daughter and sister is supposed to ask.

But some mornings, looking out the bus window at the proud tulips popping up out of the earth, I pretend that I am the one among us who can't stand babies. Ignorant thumbsuckers, uncivilized droolers, toothless malcontents. That new baby smell mothers swoon over—it's just their own soured milk. The soft, creamy skin—see how puckered and red it gets when the baby screams. To take care of a baby, you have to become accustomed to the constant sound of unhappiness; to spit-up and yellow poop; to long hours of doing nothing that requires your mental acuity, your wit, your carefully cultivated self. You will be so very tired. Once a baby is born, she will seem to expand ten times in size with her relentless needs and wants. She will care about you only in relation to herself, will claim residence in your arms and lock eyes as if to never let you go; and then, when the delicate fringe of her eyelashes finally comes to rest, you will be stuck awake, unable to turn away.

Field Notes

When Leah was sixteen, she'd seen a fetus preserved
in a jar of blue formaldehyde on her high school health
teacher's desk. "Come up and look if you want,"
Ms. Hennessey said to the class. "If you'd rather not, you
can stay where you are."

How had Ms. Hennessey gotten a fetus, and why was she
bringing it in for show and tell? She was the most peculiarly
open teacher Leah had ever had. Whenever they discussed
a difficult health issue, she seemed to have had personal
experience with it, which she'd relate to the class in the
calm, storytelling manner of the school librarian. Her
father was an alcoholic, her mother chronically depressed.
She herself had suffered from bulimia. Among her friends
were some HIV-positive, semi-recovering drug addicts.
She sported a buzz cut, wore Champion sweat suits, and
dismissed the class with a chipper "Have a nice day now,
unless you have other plans." Every once in a while, she
insisted they collectively yell out "penis" to dispel the
word's taboo power.

One by one, the students went up and peered at the jar in silence, while Ms. Hennessey sat at a student desk, flipping through a stack of papers.

"Just observe," she said lightly. "Let yourself feel whatever you feel."

Preserved at nineteen weeks of development, it was a marvelously well-formed specimen: the nubs of the fingers and toes, the tiny shells of the ears. Leah felt amazed, the way she did in biology class, when she aimed her eye through the microscope and saw an organism squiggling on the slide. Studying the fetus in its blue perfection, she admired the rightness of the human form, the evolutionary logic that had shaped it.

"That was so sad," her friend Tammy whispered when they'd returned to their seats. But Leah didn't feel sad.

"It's not a baby," she whispered back, though she couldn't say exactly what it was. A human prototype. A once-organic baby doll. A beautiful, made thing. Later, when she was asked why she'd decided to major in biology, to attend graduate school for pathology, to become a cancer researcher, she had her answers ready. Her interest in evolutionary development; her dedication to the experimental process; her desire to help in some tiny way (if she might be so bold as to suggest she could) with one of the greatest medical problems of our time. But the image that came to her was of the fetus—how fascinating it had been to peer into the jar on the desk, to see something so private, that it seemed like you weren't supposed to see, and how much she'd wanted to keep looking, to understand everything about it.

The lobby of the Biomedical Research Institute where Leah worked was cavernous and windowless with a black marble floor. People moved in and out of the revolving doors, harboring an air of covert business, while Yolanda, the receptionist, tended to the phone with its echoing ring. When Yolanda's children began coming to work with her now that school had ended, they brightened up the atmosphere of the somewhat sinister-looking lobby. Adolfo, the five-year-old, laid out memory cards on the floor, a stuffed turtle hanging out of his pocket. Nina, six, brushed her Barbie's hair. Nine-year-old Jasmine lurked by the stairwell with her deadly serious face.

Heading upstairs to her lab in the Pathology Department, Leah waved at Jasmine, who carried a small spiral notebook and was tapping her pen against the metal rings.

"Do you kill mice?" the girl demanded.

"I work with mice," Leah said. "They help us with our research. We're trying to figure out what makes people sick."

"But do the mice die?"

"Sometimes," she admitted.

"Hmmph." Jasmine regarded Leah coldly and turned away.

Leah tried to get her back. "Do you have any pets?"

Jasmine considered this. "We have Adolfo."

"Your younger brother?" Leah laughed.

"My parents won't let us. Pets are too expensive."

"If you could have a pet, though, what would it be?"

"I like dogs—big dogs. And cats, if they're friendly. My friend has a mouse. She thinks he's cute. But he has red eyes."

"Their eyes are a little freaky."

"You still shouldn't kill them."

"Some people agree with you," Leah said.

Last year there'd been a series of demonstrations outside the Institute. "All Life Is Precious," the signs said, and "Stop Human-Centrism." Her colleagues had scoffed at the demonstrators, or ignored them, but Leah stood across the street for a while and took them in. She could understand. These were people who imagined themselves in mice bodies: imprisoned, tortured, sentenced to death.

"What's in the notebook?" Leah asked. Jasmine hugged it protectively to her chest.

"I'm taking field notes. Like a biologist. I do sketches, too."

"Cool. I'd love to see them sometime, if you'd let me. I should get to work now but I'll see you later, okay?"

Jasmine said nothing. Fair enough, Leah thought. Rudeness was a kid's prerogative. She had to respect it.

In their wire cages, five to a cage, Leah's mice appeared healthy. Their coats were white and shiny. They weighed about twenty grams, the average weight for an adult mouse. Inspecting them, Leah was disappointed not to find a mouse that seemed amiss—skinny, agitated, avoiding its food. She had bred them with a mutation in their DNA that caused cancer, with the goal of learning more about how the cancer developed and spread. When a mouse was ailing, she would bring it to her lab bench and monitor the sickness until it had to be sacrificed in a chamber of CO_2. The trick was to catch the mouse at the right time. If she got to it too late and the mouse was dead, she couldn't breed the next generation with the same altered cells.

Leah sat down at her computer to work on graphing her recent data. She was tracking the extent to which the mice's cancer had metastasized to different organs: the liver, the pancreas, the colon. Manipulating data, she suddenly wanted very much to have sex with her boyfriend, whom she hadn't seen in almost a week. She pictured Greg sitting up naked in bed, awaiting her approaching hand, whose course toward his crotch was prolonged by the intrusion of x- and y-axes and statistical calculations. When her hand finally alighted, he moaned—a word that had thrilled her since she'd read it over and over again in the notorious pages of a teen novel. She said it several times to herself: he moaned, he moaned, he moaned—and she felt the word between her legs. Then she imagined Greg's attentions to her breasts and her clit, but she couldn't follow the fantasy all the way through to sex. The exact configuration of limbs wouldn't settle itself in her mind. Even a week without sex could make her think of it as a strange, near impossible act.

In eighth grade Leah's friend Mandy learned the meaning of the word *phallic,* as in "That fence post looks phallic!" "That hair spray bottle looks phallic!" Mandy had gone around delightedly pointing out that phallic symbols were everywhere, and the joke got tired long before she quit doing it. Now that Leah's period wasn't coming, the world seemed full of bawdy insinuations. The celebrity baby craze on magazine covers at the supermarket. A billboard for Planned Parenthood with a woman's curvy silhouette. Actual babies strapped to their mothers' torsos, gawking at her. She saw a coworker's diamond ring emerge from a rubber glove and remembered an elementary school jingle meant to embarrass the boy and girl paired together in the chant. In her case it had been Jared, a redheaded nerd who was said to eat earthworms. "Leah and Jared sitting in a tree. K-I-S-S-I-N-G. First comes love, then comes marriage, then comes baby in the baby carriage." A kid's recitation of adulthood, each event in its proper chronological order.

Since she'd lost her virginity at eighteen, Leah had been fastidious about safe sex. She went on the pill with her first serious boyfriend, and even then still used condoms for months, not because she didn't trust him, but because she didn't trust the pills. It wasn't rational; she believed that proper usage yielded a very high rate of effectiveness. But the image of sperm swimming past all odds was seared into her mind, from some PBS special she'd secretly watched when she was seven. With new partners she gently initiated conversations about sexual history. "Can we talk?" she'd ask, before too many clothes were shed, feeling like one of the virtuous, shadowy figures in an STD prevention ad. Eventually she went off the pill. She had headaches that her doctor thought might be related to the hormones. Also, during dry spells, she didn't like to be reminded every evening when she popped the pill that she had no need to take it.

For twelve years Leah had been safe, as safe as you could be with sex, but in her six months of dating Greg, she had several times practiced that most dubious form of birth control: withdrawal. Though she'd chastised friends who took such risks, she found the idea of it sexy, the way a tightrope act was sexy. She liked the idea of a lover extracting every bit of pleasure from inside her before hastily coming on her belly or hipbone or breasts. She'd fantasized about it: the danger, the timing, the spurt on her stomach. So when she and Greg went hiking and enjoyed a spontaneous romp on a bed of ferns, they tried it; and when they were soaping each other up in the shower once, they tried it; and on a night when Leah fumbled inside the drawer of her bedside table and pulled out an empty condom box, they tried it. And that third time—from a biological point of view—they succeeded.

In the hard rain, the windshield wipers swished at a dizzying pace. Leah pulled over by a playground and jumped out of the car. The back of her head got drenched as she bent over to throw up into a trashcan. A woman herding two toddlers under an umbrella gave her a sympathetic look. Leah drove the rest of the way to work with the radio off, afraid that the sound of earnest newscasters would trigger another bout of nausea. When she arrived at the Institute, Adolfo was pushing a plastic dump truck, Nina was whispering to a purple kangaroo, and Jasmine was monitoring the revolving door like a junior security guard.

"Hi there." Leah tried to smile. She had a flash of being seventeen years old, coming home from a party having recently puked from red wine, and hoping to convince her mother that nothing was the matter. Her mother had let her creep upstairs, but Jasmine cornered her.

"I like your shirt."

"Thanks." Leah looked down, afraid that some bit of vomit clung to the cotton.

"Look, I brought cherries." Jasmine held up a plastic bag.

"Yum," Leah gulped. "Enjoy."

She came back down a few hours later to buy gum from the 7–Eleven down the street. As she was heading out the door, Jasmine waved her notebook. "I guess I could share the field notes I wrote about you today."

Leah was suddenly nervous about what this undersized investigator might have to say about her disheveled appearance. But she believed in empirical evidence. "Sure, if you want."

Jasmine read from the notebook. "She is wearing a blue-and-green-striped shirt. I want a shirt like that. She is wearing jeans with a hole in one knee. She is wearing muddy shoes. It's raining so why didn't she wear boots? Maybe she is sick today because she looks white. I mean whiter than normal. I hope she feels better." Jasmine closed the notebook. "I might do a sketch later."

"Thanks," Leah said. "I am a little sick today."

"Is it your belly?"

"Yeah."

Jasmine reached out and petted it, as if stroking a dog. "Stop making Leah sick," she said.

Leah wanted to touch Jasmine's silky black hair, thread its softness through her fingers. She wanted to cry. She let Jasmine pet her stomach a moment longer and then hurried away, rude as a child.

Leah and Greg had met at a party. He worked as a producer for a local public radio station and played violin in a klezmer band. He smelled like honeydew melon and made excellent eye contact. Leah left the party with plans to see Greg a few nights later, and since then, without really discussing it, they'd become a couple. She was thirty; Greg was thirty-two. He was smart and nice and attractive, but if she thought about them spending the rest of their lives together, it made life feel like an endless path before her. And it wasn't that. It was an astonishing blip in the universe. She could imagine another party, another man, another love she would love more and who would love her more too, a man with whom she might one day—but not now—re-create the double helix in a variation never seen before.

Then why had she been so reckless, so shortsighted, so dumb? It was as if she'd believed the most fundamental biological mechanism of reproduction didn't apply to her.

For almost two weeks now, she'd managed to avoid Greg. He was out of town visiting family, and then she told him she was really busy at work. He didn't press her. But finally, late at night, she asked him to come over, and he showed up at her door with a bottle of wine and an innocent smile.

"I missed you," he said when they hugged and kissed, and it struck her how ignorant men were allowed to be. A man could disappear, or a woman could, and he might never even know there was a child of his in the world.

"Me too," she said. "Come sit down."

Greg held up the wine. "Pour you a glass?"

She hesitated. But what did it matter? "Sure."

Leah waited on the couch, hoping the simple task would take him a long time. As soon as she told anyone, especially Greg, it would break the spell she was spinning. She kept envisioning her body doing what women's bodies were designed to do, a process similar to the growth of cancer, but with the cells growing exactly as they should, dividing in an orderly fashion from the first fused cell. The blastula had become an embryo, the tail attached to the placenta. At four weeks it had formed arm buds, two optic nerves. It was distinctly curled, structurally similar to the embryonic state of a fish or a lizard. A pinheaded seahorse, with its forty-six human chromosomes monogramming every cell: twenty-three from the male, twenty-three from the female. It was the most common and fascinating thing.

Greg sat on the couch and handed her a glass. She set it on the coffee table.

"I need to tell you something."

"Okay."

"I'm going to have an abortion." She had meant to say *I'm pregnant,* but that declaration escaped her, at once too shocking and too tender.

"What?" Greg said. "Shit. We used condoms."

"Not always."

"I pulled out."

"It happened, Greg. It happened."

He sank his forehead into his hands and then pulled her in for a hug. "I'm sorry."

She wanted to shrug him off the way she'd wanted to shrug off the life jacket a kayaking instructor had put on her once when she was twelve. She'd known how to swim and she was good at it, but the guy insisted on strapping her in.

They drank their wine down to the last drop and didn't refill their glasses. They got into Leah's bed with their clothes on.

"You're sure about this?" Greg asked in the dark.

"Yes," she said, the truth and not the truth. There was always another life. She could let the embryo grow. Let the heart start beating, the sex take shape, the organs fully form. Let the lungs expand, expand, expand, until the baby had the capacity to breathe on its own. When it was time she would give birth—the great human struggle of the large head emerging—and there it would be, a new person, over ninety-nine percent genetically the same as everyone else, and yet that less than one percent made all the difference. In this other life, she would be the mother then, with a mother's instincts to feed and protect and love. She didn't want to have to decide; she wanted to linger in this embryonic state of suspension. That blue fetus Ms. Hennessy had brought to class almost half her life ago—she could see it still, beautifully and profoundly formed. But that had been a specimen, an unaffiliated, jarred thing. This was happening inside her, and her body made it possible, like a host sustaining a parasite. She would have to make it stop.

She made the appointment for a Friday so she could have the weekend to recover. Greg drove her to the clinic and held her hand in the waiting room. He'd been actively supportive, calling every day to see how she was doing, telling her he hoped it wouldn't hurt too much. She didn't expect him to advocate for keeping the baby and it wouldn't have changed anything if he did. Still, she felt angry—at his evident relief when she'd told him he could just remain in the waiting room; at the fact that he could sit there, reading a biography of one of the lesser presidents, fully clothed, intact.

A nurse called Leah's name, and Greg gave her hand a final squeeze. The two practitioners who would be doing the job introduced themselves, explained the procedure in gentle tones. Lying down on the table, the thin sheet covering their work, Leah found herself thinking about mice. Years ago, in high school, long before she kept droves of mice in cages and cultivated their cancer, she'd had a mouse as a pet. In her psychology class junior year, she performed simple Skinner-box experiments on this mouse, and when the behavioral psychology unit was over, she brought him home. She used to hold him in her hand, just to see up close his sleek fur, his rooting snout, his prominent ears. To feel his skittering claws surveying her palm. She hadn't yet seen a dead mouse splayed open, the head lolled back, the paws tied down to the table, all the exposed organs packed inside the tiny mammal. She was so used to it now. She knew it had to be done. Medical research was not for the sentimental. But who else, other than a biologist who worked with mice day in and day out—who observed them, dissected them, examined their cells under microscopes, who identified and analyzed their similarities to humans—could be so grateful that, as a species, mice walked the earth?

The embryonic tissue that was being removed from her uterus would be disposed of as medical waste. State law prohibited research on embryos obtained from abortions. It disgusted her to think of that valuable material simply thrown away. Didn't it matter to those fools that the polio vaccine had been developed from fetal kidney cells? She'd almost considered driving to another state out of protest. But she knew that would be a futile symbolic gesture that was not going to keep her from leaving the clinic with an emptiness inside. From tracking, for months to come, how that embryo would have grown.

Today Adolfo and Nina marched crayons back and forth across the floor, like they were soldiers in battle. Jasmine manned her post by the stairs, bent over her notebook. Today Jasmine had a question for Leah, fired off with the girl's winning abruptness. "Does everybody have to die?"

"Yes," Leah said. "That's how it is with everybody." When she was around Jasmine's age, she'd asked her mother about death, about what happened and why. Her mother had told her not to think about it, which had the opposite effect.

"I might not," Jasmine said.

"Why do you think so?"

"It's just a feeling."

Leah was back in her high school health class, hearing Ms. Hennessey's voice, so soothing in its matter-of-factness, its lack of surprise: *Let yourself feel whatever you feel.*

These past weeks, relieved of the pregnancy, she was feeling the chilly arbitrariness of life, and the great luck of it too.

"What would you do if you lived forever?" Leah asked.

"Well, first I'd go everywhere in the world and visit each place for a year," Jasmine began readily, as if she'd been preparing for someone to ask about her plans for eternal life. "Then I'd be everything you can be. I'd be an artist, a doctor, an actress, a chef, a pilot, and lots of other things. And I'd make inventions and save people and read every book in the library. But only the good ones. I'd have kids, and grandkids, and great-grandkids, and whatever comes after that to infinity. What would you do?"

"I've never considered it before," Leah said. "I guess I'd do the same thing."

Period, Ellipsis, Full Stop

On Tuesday at around noon, while Elliott was at work, Cora found a jagged circle of bright red on her white underwear, like a botched Japanese flag. Nine weeks into her pregnancy and blood was coming out of her. She sat on the toilet, knees shaking, afraid to look at the toilet paper to see how much more showed up. She'd read those parts in the pregnancy books that discussed bleeding early on, covering the bases from normal spotting, to miscarriage, to the rare but potentially life-threatening wrong turn of ectopic pregnancy. That is, from the possibility that nothing was wrong to the risk that everything was.

Cora pulled off the underwear and ran water over it in the sink, squeezing her legs together as she searched in the cabinet for a panty liner, and then hobbled into the bedroom to get a fresh pair of black underwear. Lying in bed, she thought about what Elliott might be doing right now. Cooking up event plans and budgets at his desk, his shaggy brown hair mussed into a frenzy. Leaning back in his executive chair on the phone, his hazel eyes lively and warm, as he sweet-talked a potential donor who couldn't even see the expression carefully crafted for her. Five months ago, they'd moved from Philadelphia to this small Midwestern city so that Elliott could take the helm of an up-and-coming nonprofit. It was supposed to be an exciting start to the next chapter of their lives: new jobs, their own house, a baby.

A heavy ache began to bulldoze through Cora's abdomen. The past few weeks had been full of pangs and proddings. But this was different. More ploughing and constricting than stabby and stretchy. An email popped up on her phone, and she consulted it as if it might answer the question of what was happening to her.

Dear Cora,

I have reviewed all your edits. I would appreciate the chance to debate them with you. Can we meet later this week?

Best wishes,
Kurt

She was trying to start a freelance editing business, with the hope of working on more stimulating books than she'd encountered at her previous job with a textbook company. The kind of books she liked to read— fiction, memoir, something with a strong narrative—books where the language was not governed by the need to deliver information or sell something, but was dedicated to stirring the senses, the soul. In her glummer moments, she thought that reading was the only thing she was good at, and what sort of skill was that for an adult to rely on in this world?

She'd reached out to everyone she knew, looking for potential projects; she'd made a website with a hopeful "Contact Me" link that no one had been clicking on. A few weeks ago, an acquaintance of Elliott's had introduced her to Kurt. A sixty-something retired entrepreneur, he'd written a draft of a novel and wanted it edited. "It tackles themes of justice and honor, interwoven with a great romance," he told her, when they met at a coffee shop. She was excited to edit her first novel, doubtful as she was that it would be any good. And indeed the opening chapters Kurt sent confirmed her doubts. The plot was absurd, the pacing completely off, the characters a grab bag of clichés, and the sentences like fence posts: all made the same wooden way. Still, as Cora worked with the text—tinkering with the prose, offering diplomatic critiques and cheerful pleas for more development—she felt the sheen of her own competence that she'd been missing since they'd moved and she hadn't had regular work. Now here was Kurt's response to the edits she'd sent: *I would appreciate the chance to debate them with you.* What was that supposed to mean? Didn't he know to trust that a professional's practiced eye could see what you couldn't? And that if you disagreed with some suggested changes, you just politely ignored them? It wasn't a matter for debate.

Her finger hovered over Elliott's number. If she told him

she was bleeding, he would be concerned but calm. In that manner that made him so excellent at his job, he would tell her to go see a doctor right away: he wouldn't be ordering her, just making it clear—soothingly, persuasively—that he understood what needed to be done. She hadn't even met the doctor yet; her first prenatal appointment was two weeks from now. Apparently, in early pregnancy, you weren't supposed to need anyone to monitor your progress. You could keep it to yourself, hold it inside: a familial secret, a private triumph, belly not yet giving it away. A woman's body was supposed to know exactly what to do.

She put the phone down and closed her eyes, the bloody flag of her underwear waving behind her eyelids. The last time it had scared her to see such a thing she was twelve years old. She'd been told what to expect from the booklet they handed out to the girls at school, and from the reports of her faster-developing friend Kari; both sources made menstruation seem like a sophisticated and wondrous event. It hadn't fully registered somehow that having your period meant you'd bleed actual blood, and a lot of it. Discovering her stained underwear early one morning, she felt that she must have suffered a mysterious injury in the night and her life might now be draining out of her. When Cora's mother found out what was going on, she didn't get all teary and bake a cake, like the mother in a book Cora had read. "Well, it's a drag, but I don't get PMS too bad, so hopefully you won't either," she said. "Just carry a pad with you always, and you'll be prepared." She bought Cora a pink zippered pouch to keep in her backpack and said nothing more about the matter.

For the next seventeen years, her period came every month, a dependable nuisance. At times Cora had even found it comforting: a scapegoat to blame her moodiness on, an assurance that her birth control methods were working. And then, when she and her husband of two years wanted to have a baby, she had stopped taking the pill. When her period didn't show up, the absence of blood was a reminder of its whole purpose. That monthly flow of waste product finally proved useful, stockpiled inside as nourishment for a new life, her body the womanly wonder described in the *For Girls Only* booklet after all.

Cora pulled her laptop off the nightstand and googled *bleeding pregnancy nine weeks.* The internet responded with its typical outpouring. The generically informative articles that collectively revealed nothing, mixed in with the queries and pleas and stories that told too much: the play-by-play of anxiety and confusion and prayer and nightmare and everything-turned-out-okay and my-life-is-ruined. The bad grammar and misspellings and weird punctuation and melodrama that was for the most part numbing, but sometimes some anonymous person's naked account of their experience could get to you, and you might weep, without being sure whether you were weeping for this anonymous person or for yourself. Cora immersed herself in it for almost an hour, toggling between empathy and panic, and then she made herself go to the bathroom, where she found a splotch of blood on the panty liner, a smaller blot than last time. The tainted underwear was still in the sink. She dropped it in the trash and went back to bed.

Unless things got worse, she would wait and call the doctor tomorrow. Would count herself in the camp of first-trimester women for whom bleeding was just a symptom of pregnancy, not of its imminent end. The ones who reported happy news to the online forums: *All's well! Alive and kicking! Just a bit of spotting, nothing more.* Not the others, not the sad ones, the desperate ones. She was going to close up her computer and shut those women away inside it. But there was still the matter of Kurt to attend to. She clicked on his email and donned a pleasant, casual-professional tone, while her uterus throbbed.

Dear Kurt,

I'd be happy to meet. How about Friday at 3:00, at the Whole Bean again? There's a slight chance I might have to reschedule, but if so, of course I'll let you know. Looking forward to talking.

Best,
Cora

Then she drove to Walgreens for maxi pads, which she hadn't worn since she'd learned to use tampons at fifteen, but if you bled during pregnancy, the internet had just taught her, you weren't supposed to use a tampon. The elderly cashier who rang up Cora's purchase put the maxi pads in a plastic bag and said, "Here you are, sweetie," as if she were tendering sympathy.

When Elliott got home, they had a dinner of baked potatoes and steamed vegetables, the only things Cora could bring herself to prepare and eat. He was full of work gossip, a welcome distraction, but also a trigger for her jealousy: she didn't have colleagues, she didn't have complicated projects she was trying to get off the ground. Elliott asked how her day was, and she hesitated before telling him about the email from Kurt.

"So you'll debate him," Elliott said. "No big deal. Your arguments will be stronger than his, and either he'll realize that or he won't. His problem, not yours. It's his book."

"But maybe it's my fault if I don't communicate things in a way that gets him to understand."

"That's not in your control. Think about it. You show a climate change denier solid evidence of the rise in global temperature and warming oceans and shrinking polar ice sheets—and they're like, then why was it so cold last winter?"

He was right of course. But she was not in the mood for him to be right; she was intent on feeling bad and she wasn't going to let him stop her.

She went to bed early while Elliott watched TV in the living room. Virtuous TV: a documentary special about wildfires. She hadn't told him about the blood, the cramping, the internet sisters she'd sought out and then tried to forget. He would be on her about that too, and even though it would be out of care, she didn't want to have to reveal how her body might be failing both of them. In the bed that felt both luxuriously expansive and lonely without him in it, she pressed her legs together, trying to imagine that if she clenched tight enough, nothing could spill out between them. As if she could say sternly, *You're not going anywhere young lady, young man, whoever you are*—and that would be that—the matter decided through her own sheer determination to keep everything inside.

The next morning, after Elliott left for work, Cora called and described her symptoms in response to the nurse's questions. *How much bleeding? A teaspoon or a tablespoon's worth or more?* About a teaspoon, Cora guessed. *Pain? Cramping?* Yes, but worse yesterday than today. She was glad not to be asked to quantify the pain on a scale of one to ten, which always struck her as more of a measurement of stoicism or self-pity than pain itself. The nurse was noncommittal. Cora could come in today; she could come in a few days from now. They scheduled an appointment for Monday, after the meeting with Kurt, after she'd have the weekend to talk with Elliott about what was going on—or not, depending on how things went.

And now what to do? She felt too stuck in her own reality to enjoy where a book might take her. She could call a friend, but she hadn't told anyone yet that she was pregnant, and didn't want to have to conceal her current uncertainty. She could do errands. Over the past month, she'd started thinking of the baby as a silent companion, accompanying her to the grocery store, the library, the bank—these ordinary places made slightly more interesting by pretending that someone else was experiencing them with her.

She made herself put on a jacket and go out for a walk. On this late September afternoon, the trees ran the gamut from a still-full leafy green, to lion's-mane yellow, to the circuslike surprise of orangey-red. Cora didn't know anything about trees, didn't know their names. But on a residential street near her house, she identified a particular tree that could have been included in a field guide to her life. That species of tree had stood in a courtyard inside her high school: a serene pocket amid the teen clamor. She'd never seen anyone in the courtyard, but one day during her free period, in the fall of junior year, she tried the door and it opened. A bench flanked by those glorious trees called out to her to lie down there and read. All through that fall, she lifted nineteenth-century novels up to the sky—*Tess of the d'Urbervilles, Wuthering Heights, Jane Eyre*—and the golden span of leaves formed a frame around the book. The combination of the beautiful tree and the beautiful book almost made her feel lifted out of her loneliness. She couldn't remember babyhood, of course, what it was like to have her parents tote her around, to cling to their animal warmth. It was at sixteen years old, it seemed to her, that she most wanted to be held.

In winter she went out to the courtyard in a wool coat and gloves, the naked branches shining like bones. By spring, when the trees were budding, other students had pushed open the door, and the place was no longer hers. Sometimes Elliott Tishman—a senior, conventionally cute, effortlessly popular, the student body vice president—sat on the opposite bench with his girlfriend, Darcy, a strawberry blonde with a throaty laugh. Cora watched Darcy draw circles on Elliott's thighs with her red fingernails while he settled his arms back behind his head and closed his eyes. The book felt heavy in Cora's hands; she read without reading.

Six years later, after she'd graduated from college, she found herself next to him at the makeshift bar of an apartment in downtown Philadelphia. "You're Elliott, right?" she said.

"I'm sorry," he said. "Have we met?"

"I wouldn't expect you to recognize me. I was a year behind you at Aberdeen."

"Oh, I guess I must have been too mature to notice you."

"Yeah," she laughed. "Also, I didn't really talk to anybody in high school."

"Above it all, huh?"

"No, the opposite. I didn't think anyone would be interested in me."

"Aw, that couldn't have been true," he said, and for the first time, she thought maybe that was right.

"Well anyway, Mr. Vice President, can I make you a cocktail?"

She'd figured out how to flirt in college. Though she would never be a talker or a toucher—one of those women adept at stroking men with voice or hands—she was quick and light with a conversational volley. It was like being good at writing papers: efficiently seizing the reader's attention and leading him along.

"I'd love a cocktail," Elliott said.

Later, when people asked how they'd met, Cora would describe him as a high school crush. "He wasn't aware of my existence back then," she said. "I had to bide my time, get him drunk on whiskey sours." And Elliott would look pleased, basking in the story of having been the one pursued. Cora had learned that you could package your insecurities as self-deprecation, and that this could be charming. And she was learning, five years into their relationship, how insecurity continued to stick with her, did not dissolve because the boy she'd wanted had asked, "What would you think about getting married?"; had looked into her eyes when they had unprotected sex for the first time and said, "Maybe we'll make a baby. Can you believe it?"

Her neighborhood was staunchly residential, with three-story houses attached to generous lawns. *A great place to raise kids*—how many times had she heard that already? Cora found herself differentiating the houses not by her usual criteria—whether they appeared, from the outside anyway, better or worse than her own—but according to whether they contained signs of children or not. A swing hanging from a tree branch, toddler car left in the grass, stroller on the porch, construction paper creations taped to the windows, toys visible inside. The rock garden in front of one house was teeming with plastic rats and spiders: an infestation of beady eyes, twirly tails, wink-wink creepiness. It could go either way with that one—an adult's Halloween spirit, a kid's practical joke. Cora would like to have consulted with the baby, to see what he or she thought of it, but the baby wasn't taking lawn decor questions. It was preoccupied with the big ontological stuff: *to be or not to be;* at any moment it could slip out of this world as clotted blood and fine tissue.

Thursday night in bed, Elliott squeezed her against his bare chest, the way he did when they were likely to have sex soon. She froze, trying to figure out what to do. During her period, a little blood didn't stop him. He'd get a towel to protect the sheet, and he licked her with his usual fervor, and then carefully eased the tampon out and set it on the nightstand. And why shouldn't he? Men left their own sticky secretions on women all the time. Why should menstrual blood be more taboo than semen? Why should it be seen, why should she herself sometimes see it, as disgusting? Still, his nonchalance about it felt like a validation, a benediction of that basic female function essential to life, or maybe an expression of love for her in particular. But if you might be having a miscarriage, you shouldn't have sex—the internet and the nurse had both said this, though common sense implied as much. She certainly didn't feel like doing it. If she told him she didn't want to, though, without telling him the reason, her trepidation would turn into loneliness, and her deception would become sadness. She did not want to be lonely and sad in bed with her half-naked husband.

"Something might be wrong," she said.

His tight squeeze loosened. "What do you mean?"

"I'm bleeding a little."

"Oh. What does that . . . what do you think is going on?"

"I don't know. It could be nothing. Or. It's really common. I mean, the numbers aren't clear, but it could be as high as twenty percent of pregnancies that end in—"

"No." She could see him wince in the dark. "When did this start? Why didn't you tell me?"

"I was hoping it was just—some women do bleed in early pregnancy."

"How do you find out for sure?"

"I have an appointment on Monday and then they'll, I guess they'll see."

She lay loosely in his arms, and in the silence before he began to comfort her, she could feel how she'd hurt him; and she wanted to hug him and apologize and make him feel how much she loved him, and she wanted him to stay hurt.

Kurt was already at a table when Cora got to the café, the printed pages of his manuscript stacked next to a coffee cup. He was dressed as if for a business meeting, in a pinstriped shirt and suit jacket. Cora ordered the "calm chamomile" tea and brought it over, summoning up her professional self. "The weather's been so nice," she said. "When does it start to get cold here?"

"Sometime in November it'll hit you," Kurt said. "Listen, I'm not much for small talk. What do you think of the book so far?"

"It's interesting," she fumbled. "A lot of action, lots of stuff going on. Passionate characters."

"Yes, Maurice is passionate about everything. His work, his family, his belief that justice must be done. So why did you take issue with this, here, in the scene where he proposes to Larissa?" Kurt rifled through the pages. "You said, 'Heavy-handed. Consider toning down emotion to sharpen and particularize the characters in this pivotal moment.'"

"Right."

"But that's Maurice. That's his character. So how am I supposed to show him as an emotional guy if I cut down on the emotion?"

She tried to explain how readers tended to pull back when characters were being melodramatic—crying and shouting from rooftops and making passionate declarations to each other. "Since the writer seems to be telling you to feel so much, there isn't room to bring your own sympathies to it. See what I mean?"

Kurt frowned. "But doesn't that depend on the reader? Some people are afraid to engage on an intense emotional level."

"I don't think that's the issue. If you reined in the

sentimental language here, and in other places, you could actually generate more emotion for these characters."

"We might have to agree to disagree," Kurt said. "Let's take something else. You deleted all of my ellipses." He read again from her comments on the manuscript: " 'Why not just end the sentence? Period, full stop. Or write what it is that you're wanting to say.' Now my understanding is that an ellipsis lets the reader read between the lines, use his imagination. Isn't that what you were just suggesting I do?"

"Not really," she said, trying to keep her composure, to explain how an ellipsis was a kind of cop-out. To hint at more without actually delivering the goods was to hide behind punctuation, to let an evasion stand in for the truth rather than writing it cold, writing it harsh, writing it thorny and complicated.

It was the universal law of things getting worse over the weekend, when the doctors' office was closed and wouldn't open again till Monday morning. Cora lay on the couch, pressing a hot water bottle to her throbbing abdomen, the thick maxi pad sticky between her legs. Elliott was cautiously attentive, gently massaging her shoulders. When he asked how the meeting with Kurt had gone, she told him Kurt had given her a check for the work she'd done so far. She told him her feedback hadn't gone over that well, without describing how the guy had argued with her for an hour, twisting her editorial suggestions around with his faulty logic and misguided sense of aesthetics. Elliott, were he dealing with Kurt in some capacity at work, would have shrugged him off, but it wasn't so easy for her to ignore. Her sense of her own professional authority stood on a pedestal built out of paper, and with a few words, someone could blow it down. Her first shot at editing a novel had failed.

In the bathroom she found more dark red, angry-looking clotted blood. So was this it, in earnest now? How much was going to come out, and would it be too much? *Miscarriage. Hemorrhage.* Both words shadowy and sinister—womanly in the worst way. The nurse had told her to call Labor and Delivery Triage at the hospital if the bleeding got too heavy. They knew how to deal with the complications of pregnancy at any point. But it was *Labor and Delivery,* Cora thought. Designed for full-term pregnant women, bursting with babies about to be born. It seemed cruel: the new mother side by side with the no-not-now mother, the not-expectant-anymore mother.

By Saturday night the bleeding had slowed down again, the cramping flattened out into a dull pelvic ache. Goddamn ellipsis.

On Sunday afternoon an email arrived from Kurt.

Dear Cora,

After some thought, I'm afraid I've come to the conclusion that we just aren't the best match. So I won't continue with

*your services, though I thank you for offering your unique
perspective.*

Best wishes,
Kurt

"He's not worth your time," Elliott said. "Don't worry
about it. It doesn't matter."

"That's easy for you to say," she exploded. "I don't have a
job here. I have nothing. That fucking guy was all I had."

She could see Elliott was thinking of saying something
and holding his tongue. She was ashamed of her outburst
but could not bring herself to soften it with an apology or a
qualification. Elliott brought her a cup of tea, and then left
her on the couch.

O n Monday morning, Elliott drove her to the doctor's
office. The pink-lipsticked receptionist took Cora's
name, typed something, and then swiveled around to a
file cabinet, producing a folder and a book, *Our Bodies,
Ourselves: Pregnancy and Birth.* Cora recoiled at the cover:
a lineup of smiling women holding babies. "Why are you
giving me this?"

"It's complimentary for all maternity patients," the
receptionist said, unfazed.

Cora turned toward the waiting room where Elliott
was sitting and looking up at her, and silently handed
him the book. She opened the folder to find an array of

informational sheets and pamphlets: *Manage Your Birth Plan, Consider Cord Blood Donation, Prenatal Yoga Classes.* It was like giving a diabetic a bunch of recipes for cookies and cakes.

In the examination room, she stripped from the waist down and wrapped the thin sheet around herself. Elliott, in a chair next to a diagram of the female reproductive system, looked so thoroughly dressed in his work clothes: khaki pants with a leather belt cinching a purple-checked button-down, probably the first piece of clothing she'd ever bought for him, a birthday present four years ago. She remembered wandering through the racks in the men's department at Nordstrom, thumbing the strangely large masculine clothing, savoring the pleasure of buying a shirt for her lover. "I'm a little jealous," Elliott had said about the fact that she, as a woman, could be capable of growing a baby. But she wondered whether, given the opportunity, he would really prefer to be the one carrying it for nine months rather than to remain as he was, with his tailored shirt tucked neatly into his trim pants, having already played his brief part, nothing dependent on him anymore.

Dr. Krish came in and shook their hands; she was a gray-haired woman about Cora's mother's age. Cora had always stood in awe of doctors, though she'd certainly never wanted to be one. They dealt with people's pain, with the harsh realities of the body; they delivered awful news. Perhaps being an editor was a lesser profession, nitpicky and inessential—but at least the worst news she had to deliver was that the writer could do a better job with his words.

She lay with her legs splayed apart, and the doctor's gloved hands reached up inside. "The cervix is open," Dr. Krish said, a statement that sounded neutral, perhaps even positive in terms of a visceral response, open = good, but in pregnancy the gates were supposed to be shut tight, like the cabin door of an airplane, until the safe landing, the joyful arrival.

"I'm going to do an ultrasound to see what's going on," the doctor said calmly, and Cora thought of the worried women online who'd turned out to still be pregnant in the end, whose babies showed up on ultrasounds and proved their anxious mothers wrong—they weren't gone, weren't vanished into nothing. She couldn't decipher the images that appeared on the screen in front of her, except to recognize that the machine kept zooming in on something: an asteroid blob in a lunar landscape.

"It's been ten weeks since your last period, yes?" the doctor asked, and Cora nodded.

"It looks like the fetus is measuring seven weeks. Most likely it stopped growing then and has taken some time to descend. That's quite common."

The doctor paused. "I'm very sorry. We could do a D&C and remove it immediately if you want, but I don't think it's necessary. You should be fine waiting at home, if you feel comfortable with that. There's also a suppository I could prescribe that's likely to move things along more quickly.

"If it's any comfort, a miscarriage is usually the body's way of ending a pregnancy that was never going to be viable. At this point, I don't see that it should affect your future chances of conceiving and carrying through to term."

In the parking lot, they sat in the car holding hands, like a very young couple. It felt more intimate than an embrace. "I guess it shouldn't matter now, but I was hurt that you didn't tell me right away, when you started bleeding," Elliott said.

"I know," Cora said. "I'm sorry."

"So why didn't you?"

"There isn't a good reason. I wasn't sure what was going on. I was scared. I was trying to pretend it wasn't happening. And I didn't want you to be disappointed."

"You don't need to protect me," he said.

Of course, she had also been protecting herself. Sometimes she felt as if she were still lying alone on that high school bench, clinging to an imaginary romance full of passion (the kind of book Kurt had wanted to write perhaps, but it was so damn hard to pull off), while Elliott and Darcy pressed against each other on the opposite bench. Even though that time was long past. Even though he'd chosen her. And had said one night, a week or so after they'd learned she was pregnant, "I was thinking, if you hadn't made me a drink, we wouldn't be here, having a baby together. So thanks for that drink."

Pain woke her up in the middle of the night, forced her out of bed doubled over, into the bathroom, where she pulled off her pajama bottoms. The misoprostol she'd inserted in her vagina before bed must be working then, moving things along, as the doctor had said. The on-and-off discomfort of the past week had become an urgent wrenching feeling, like something was trying to extricate itself. The fifteen minutes of online research she'd allowed herself revealed that the medication was often prescribed for do-it-yourself abortions. Somewhere, at this moment, another woman cringed on a toilet, praying that what she'd never wanted to happen would end here and now. In a hospital somewhere, a woman was laboring to push out a baby she already knew was dead. And a woman who hadn't suspected that anything was wrong was wondering why it had emerged from her body without a sound, why she wasn't hearing the inevitable crying of a naked newborn, stunned by sudden light and cold.

Cora heard a pop, felt a slippery shape, like an egg—she was shocked at the obviousness of it—slide out of her, and what followed was clear relief, a sense of having eliminated the obstruction. She thought about waking Elliott up and telling him, calling him into the bathroom with her as witness. But she realized she didn't want a witness. After a while she got up and flushed the toilet without looking, though she wondered what it would be like to be the sort of person who would want to see, whose curiosity would overtake her fear.

When had it started, where had it come from—the belief that she had to keep all her muck, her mistakes, her failures hidden until some dream of a magical time when she might be old enough, graceful enough, smart enough, to leave all of that behind? As if perfection were a class you could sign up for, but every time she attempted to register, it was already filled to capacity. As if her marriage to Elliott was a competition she was losing, or some fraudulent scheme she'd pulled off, and when it was uncovered, he wouldn't want to be with her after all. As if she wasn't getting editing work because people had become such good writers now, they didn't need editors anymore. They were sailing through reports and academic treatises, memoirs and novels—arriving at the last page and boom, done. Sentences, paragraphs, whole chapters: everything emerging fresh in the fittest incarnation of itself. Each punctuation mark beautifully in service to the effortless flow of syntax, each word the best possible word. As if you could set out to do something and get it right the first time, as if the whole of life wasn't about trying again.

White Carnations

We didn't have mothers anymore, nor were we mothers ourselves, so we got together on Mother's Day at a down-and-out pub frequented by gay men and regular drunks. There weren't any mothers there, as far as we could tell, and the day gave us that kind of radar. We knew who was a mother and who wasn't. It was the third anniversary of our early May outing, and we all showed up on time, at two o'clock on this sunstruck afternoon, as if we couldn't wait to get inside where it felt dark and smoky, even though smoking had been banned in New York City bars and restaurants for several years now.

The tradition started with Elaine and Lara, who worked together at a museum. When Elaine came back to work after her mother died, Lara took her out for a fancy lunch and made her weep over her plate of hazelnut-crusted salmon, followed by chocolate turtle cake with caramel beurre salé. Sometime after that, Elaine met Anne, a social worker, at a fund-raiser, and they ended up discussing how they both were motherless now.

Then Lara and I met at a party. It was the first party I had gone to since my mother's death. I wore a red strapless dress and felt insanely cheerful and dangerously cavalier. I talked to women about bikini waxing and bed bugs. I found a way to touch every man I met: hand, shoulder, hip. At the punch bowl Lara introduced herself.

"What do you do?" Lara asked. I told her that I did program administration for a ballet school, where I used to dance myself. Before I had time to reciprocate the question, she asked, "And what do your parents do?" The snobbery surprised me from this woman in jeans and a ponytail, but I was prepared for all questions that night, prepared to hold myself apart from whatever was asked of me.

"I don't know my father, and my mother is dead."

"Yes," Lara said.

I didn't go home with a man that night. I drank spiked punch with Lara, who, it turned out, was not snobbish about pedigree or profession. Parental loss was her stock-in-trade.

So when Mother's Day came around, with its bouquets and dinner specials, Elaine invited Anne, and Lara invited me, and there were four of us. But I imagined that our numbers were secretly legion, that in windowless joints throughout the city, huddled groups of women gathered, not a mother among them. We weren't quite commemorating, and we weren't quite commiserating, though we weren't in denial either. We spent hours together in the hard wooden booth, and we ate and drank, talked and laughed, and it was a kind of fun fueled by each of our particular experiences of death.

For Elaine's mother it was Alzheimer's. At the end, as if to prove to Elaine that she'd always favored her younger daughter, she could remember the name Janice, but not Elaine, though Elaine was the one who visited her mother more often, who had to explain over and over again why she couldn't go back to her sweet little childhood house with the Victory Garden she and her mother and sisters had planted. Anne's mother had died of cancer, the super fast kind, for which the relatives flew in right away to say goodbye. And Lara's mother killed herself many years ago. Lara was twelve, away at camp for the summer. One morning she dropped a letter to her mother in the camp mailbox. That afternoon, her uncle came to take her home. The letter arrived a few days later. Lara retrieved it from the mailbox, lit a match, and burned it. When the paper was consumed, she let the flame burn her skin.

When you think about it afterward, there is always something, in addition to the death, that marks the occasion. My mother was killed in a car accident three and a half years ago. Taxi drivers are known for their death-defying skills: you lurch and you cringe, but you get to where you're going sooner than the other guys on the road, except in my mother's case. And what else happened earlier that day? I sat in my office at the ballet school and watched the gingko leaves glide off the tree outside my window, the way gingko trees divest themselves, stunningly, all at once.

At the pub, Lara and I sat on one side of the booth, Anne and Elaine on the other. I was the youngest at twenty-six, and Lara, thirty-three, was the second youngest. We both favored eyeliner that made our eyes seem darker and not entirely trustworthy. We wore jeans that skinnied our already skinny legs. Elaine was fifty-two, with the skin of a woman who swore by an excellent facial cream, her hair a pretty, well-maintained white. Anne was a determined blonde at forty, good-looking in a hard way, with the polished directness of an anchorwoman. Lara's mother and my own had died before their time, by choice and by accident, and Elaine and Anne's mothers had died in their seventies, a reasonable age to go. But all of us, their daughters, wanted to make ourselves attractive not just for partners or lovers or coworkers or one another. When we looked in the mirror, we wanted to place ourselves far away from our mothers' fate.

Soon my body would escape the tight control I'd always imposed as a dancer. It had already begun, with inflated breasts and a slight slackening of my belly. I was three months pregnant, and though, five weeks earlier, I'd gone to an abortion clinic, I had left still pregnant. When I was stretched out on the table, waiting for the doctor, I was expecting a woman. I'd always had female doctors and I preferred it that way. When men tended to my body, I wanted it to be for pleasure. Women were the clinicians, women older than I was, who had chosen this depressing profession that seemed the opposite of dance. Doctors worked with the body immobilized, the body unhealthy and unbeautiful. I felt sorry for them in their white coats and sensible shoes.

The doctor came in. "Hi, Karyn," he said amiably, as if he knew me. He was tall, fiftyish, with grayish brown hair, good-looking in a mild way. With the nurse's help, he began to prepare his instruments. Because I had never known my father, it was my habit to recognize him in a man of a certain age. His features, his voice, whatever task or gesture his hands were engaged in—I studied them all. I looked enough like my mother that lack of resemblance did not disqualify a man. I didn't expect my father to be like me; I expected him to be as strange and remote as he was to my life. And vis-à-vis the inevitable converging paths of lost parents and children, well-documented in fairy tales and movies, here he was: my seventh-grade biology teacher, a proctor at the SATs, the college dance department advisor, a docent at the Met, the super of my apartment building, the doctor who was about to perform my abortion.

He sat down by my stirruped feet, his gloved hands outstretched. "First I'm going to touch your cervix. It shouldn't hurt. You'll just feel some pressure." I dug my nails into my palms. No, it didn't hurt. I had heard that the cervix softened during pregnancy, and I wondered what that softness felt like to a practiced hand. The doctor disengaged himself. I watched his moderately handsome competence and I felt compelled to stop it.

"I'm sorry." I scooted up the table to an upright position. "I have to go."

The nurse looked at the doctor, and I wondered how common last-minute defections were, and if they scored it as a point for the anti-abortion gang.

"Are you sure?" the doctor asked.

"Yes," I lied, blazing with embarrassment and freedom. I was sure I wouldn't see him again, though perhaps I would make an appointment somewhere else, ask for a female doctor, keep my eyes shut.

"Okay," he said, with a slight edge to his voice, the edge I imagined a father would have with his squirming child, reprimanding her: and why didn't you go to the bathroom earlier, when I asked if you needed to? "We'll leave you to get dressed."

I let time pass. I did not exactly say to myself, I will keep this baby. I was waiting to see what would happen. In the early mornings I ran in the park, around the murky reservoir, fighting off exhaustion. At work I watched girls in leotards and tights, girls with sweet, silky skin practicing before class. I met friends for dinner and told them I was taking antibiotics and couldn't drink. I thought of the doctor, who had known my secret and didn't care, and, walking down the street, I fixated on other men of fifty or so who, allowing for a great accident of time and place, could have brought me into being, unbeknownst to them. I had always seen my father everywhere, but my mother I had not seen since a week before her death.

The pub menus were stained and familiar, with their selection of unwholesome food: bacon-cheese melt, clam chowder, fish and chips. The closest you could get to healthy was Caesar salad. Today we all agreed to enjoy things that tasted great and bad at the same time, that left us feeling bloated and satisfied.

"My neighbor gave me a white carnation this morning," Anne said. "A nice gesture, but you know."

"Ugh," went Elaine.

"Why aren't you wearing it in your buttonhole?" Lara mocked.

"I don't get it," I said.

"Carnations—the Mother's Day flower," Lara said. "Red for the living. White for the purity of a dead mother's love."

I wondered aloud how Mother's Day got started anyway, and Anne said that a woman named Anna Jarvis had wanted to create a memorial to her mother. "It caught on and was declared a national holiday in 1914. But she got disgusted with it. The commercialism, Hallmark and chocolates— you know the whole bit. She ended up spending her family inheritance campaigning against Mother's Day and died in poverty. She never married, never had children."

Anne had been trying to get pregnant for years. She filled us in on her methods: basal thermometers, clomiphene, two rounds of IVF. She wanted a baby so badly, and I found the distressed energy she poured into the baby-making project unappealing, a mark against her for being so earnest and unsexy. It had bothered me to think of her and her husband having sex on designated days in the missionary position to allow the sperm the shortest trip to the egg—or worse, making regular visits to the fertility clinic, where sex was a matter of extracting and inserting the necessary material. Now I sat across from her, my womb occupied by an inhabitant I hadn't meant to encourage. Looking at Anne's carefully concealed frown lines, I felt guilty for my immature attitude. If that was what they wanted, why shouldn't they do everything to try to have a child?

The waiter arrived with our drinks. A gin and tonic, a Manhattan, a Molson, and a root beer. I was prepared with my antibiotics excuse, but no one commented. Elaine began talking about her mother.

"Did I tell you she didn't even recognize herself in the mirror? But when she looked at an old photo of herself as a young woman—*oh yeah, that's me.* Smooth skin, long hair, and smiling on a bicycle seat. I could never figure out if she knew it was from the past, or if she actually thought that was what she looked like."

"When she saw herself in the mirror, who did she think it was?" Lara asked.

"Just some old lady, I think. Another woman who happened to be in the room, like a roommate. But the one good thing about it all was that as soon as she started losing her memory, she didn't care who Nancy was anymore. It seemed plausible to her that Nance was just a friend I'd invited over. Then eventually she didn't recognize either of us. So maybe we should give all the homophobes just a little bit of Alzheimer's."

Elaine and Nancy had been together for years, as had Anne and Robert. It was incumbent upon Lara and me to provide the dating stories. When she wasn't at parties, bobbing for orphans, Lara was online. She liked the way you could scrutinize a guy, pore over photos and read into chats, before actually meeting him. My boyfriends, flings, and one-night stands were usually men I met by dancing with them, feeling first the tension in their arms, the concentration or abandon of their faces near mine. Since I'd stopped dancing ballet in college, I went to clubs with bump-and-grind music. More and more, I went alone. Sometimes I brought men home, and who was around to tell me that I shouldn't?

In January I'd met Philippe that way. He wasn't a great dancer, but he was determined, keeping up with me for three hours, his clammy fingers stuck in mine. He was French, from Nice or Nantes, I forgot which. A gawkily handsome man, he would probably seem a boy until he was forty, and then he'd start retreating into bony limbs and wrinkles.

"Do you live here?" he asked, when it was clear that we were dancing with each other and wanted to keep on doing it.

"You might say that," I said. "I come here often."

"But in New York, do you live?" I liked his accent. I liked that it made him seem both sophisticated and unsure.

"Yes," I said. "For my whole life."

"Great. Do you love it?"

"I try to love it," I said, but I think the qualification was lost on him.

Philippe was visiting the East Coast, with a backpack and an English pocket dictionary. He'd gone to D.C. and Philadelphia. After New York, he was on to Boston and Vermont.

"Vermont in January. You know it'll be really cold."

"Yes, all the snow. Like a fairy tale. I want to see it." He pulled me closer, and I thought of the romance: New York for the first time. And I would be a girl he had met there, who used to be a dancer, and who danced him into her bed.

Since my mother had died and left me some money, I could afford to have my own place. It was on the border of the Upper West Side and Harlem, in a building with a Christmas tree in the lobby six months out of the year. In the elevator there was a black-and-white framed picture of somebody's son from long ago, with pomaded hair and pink cheeks painted on. My apartment was white and empty, bare walls, no rugs on the hardwoods, though I'd been told when I moved in that New York City law required carpeting on eighty percent of the floors. When he came up occasionally to fix my toilet, the landlord glanced around but didn't comment. I kept the place clean and the neighbors didn't complain. In the elevator we smiled at each other and then studied the door. A storage unit held most of the things I'd saved from my mother's apartment. An old oak stereo and boxes of records, dreamy folk songs I used to twirl to as a little girl. A series of antique lamps we'd hauled onto the subway. An armchair she settled into in the evenings. I sometimes found her there in the morning, with a mystery novel nearing the end of its mystery, her thigh a prominent bookmark. Sometimes I thought about renting a truck and furnishing my apartment with those things that were gathering dust in storage. But I left them there. I had always loved the gleaming bareness of the dance studio, free of the oppressiveness of stuff. No stuff could survive on the dance floor. It would be pliéd and pas de deuxed and jetéd aside.

My bed was high and firm and piled with white blankets. Philippe pulled me on top of him. "You are all so pretty," he said.

This moment when sex began with an almost stranger was always something of a puzzlement. Why do this, of all things, with a man whose name was still new on my tongue? But by then it was too late. Our limbs were artfully arranged, our chests pressed together, our mouths hovering near each other with embattled breath. I liked it. I wanted it. If on some level I also disapproved, so be it. I had trained for years to keep my body in alignment, to follow strict orders, to perform on command. Let my mind stumble and stagger about. Let it simper and second-guess. My body would carry on with its amorous work.

Still, I wasn't such an idiot that I didn't use condoms. The top drawer of my nightstand was reserved for only an

eye pillow and a box of Trojans. But Philippe couldn't seem
to manage with one on. We spent a while trying. Finally,
I threw it aside.

"Is it okay?" he asked. For three years, whenever
someone asked if I was okay, I thought of my mother.
Her taxi had crashed into a guardrail, and she died on the
shoulder of the Cross Bronx Expressway at forty-five years
old. How could things be okay?

I kissed Philippe's tender neck. "Yes," I whispered. I
trusted his polite and eager foreignness, and sex was always
a diversionary gamble anyway. I just didn't really care.

At the pub, we had consumed seven alcoholic drinks,
two root beers, and an assortment of things sauce-
smothered and fried.

"Okay, last one," Anne said, plucking an onion ring
from Lara's plate. "We have to go to dinner with Robert's
parents tonight."

"Can't you get out of it? Tell them you need to see a
sick friend. After a few more beers, I'll throw up for you,"
Elaine said.

"You know what my mother-in-law would say? 'She wants
to see *you,* this sick friend? You're a doctor now? What
happened to the social work?' The way she says *social work,*
it's like I'm planning parties. Her faith in doctors is insane.
According to her I just haven't gone to the doctor enough—
that's why I can't have kids. You find a good doctor, and you

go to him, and you keep on going to him until he fixes you. Unless you have cancer, and then there's no hope."

Anne ate another onion ring. "But I've been saving my good news. We put an application in with an adoption agency in China. They approved it last week."

We all agreed this was great and clinked our glasses with Anne's.

"Do you know how long it might take?" Lara asked.

"It could be a month. It could be six months. We have to be ready to buy a ticket to China. They tell you when to come, and then they send you on a tour with these other prospective parents. It's this weird vacation where you get a baby prize at the end."

I let Lara and Elaine continue to ask the questions. Last Mother's Day Anne and I had clashed over adoption. She was struggling through her second round of IVF, and I wanted to know whether she was considering adopting. "Yes, of course," she said coldly. But they really wanted their own baby. I pressed her on it. Why such attachment to your own genetic lineage? I didn't mean to be self-righteous or accusatory. My interest in this topic was philosophical. Wasn't motherhood essentially a matter of care? Was origin so important? True, I had fantasized all my life about finding my father. But wasn't that because I didn't have any father at all?

"Okay, Karyn," Anne had said. "You make a good case. But do me a favor? Let me have my fantasy. Let me have it until I'm out of patience and stamina and spirit, which will happen soon, and then maybe I'll come around to your point of view."

I felt like I'd been put in my place by a teacher or a mother, though not by my mother, who wouldn't be so direct. But then, I hadn't pushed her the way I pushed Anne. I had never asked her what she thought motherhood was. I had never asked her for my father's name. In the following year, Anne and I saw each other at a few different social occasions. We weren't friends exactly. There was formality and tension, a kind of tightly controlled uncertainty between us, the kind that makes you think either you'll never connect with this person, or you will eventually, in a deep and inextricable way.

"They're all girls, of course," Anne said about the Chinese babies. "I've always wanted a girl. I remember thinking at nine or so, in an extreme boy-hating stage, maybe I'll adopt a baby when I'm older so I won't get stuck with a stupid boy. I was always planning ahead."

"Girls are the best," Elaine said.

"Girls are the smartest," Lara said.

It was hard to tell how happy Anne was about the prospect of adoption. But then, we weren't a happy bunch. We descended into this below-street-level pub on Mother's Day, holding our losses close, though how much did they really have to do with the way we met the world? Whatever influences our mothers had on us, that work had been done long ago. And though we had our moments of tunneling into the past with hard hat and headlamp, for the most part, out of loyalty and love, fear and denial, we didn't want to think about how our mothers had raised us.

What I had thought about a lot since my mother's death was the story of how she came to be my mother. That is, from a child's perspective, how she came to be herself. I knew the story from bits she had told me over the years and from the narrative license of my own imagination.

Elizabeth Rylant grew up on a farm in Idaho. She was the only child of older parents who were surprised when she finally came along. They'd resigned themselves to calves and chicks and kittens for babies. But Elizabeth was born, and she was a restless child, racing through her chores and startling the animals. She watched the Times Square New Year's Eve celebration on TV every year. "The Big Apple," she wrote for a fourth grade social studies report. "It doesn't have apple trees and it's actually not that big. But seven million people live inside it. When I grow up, I will be one of them." Her parents smiled at her dream. What she didn't know, apart from how impossibly expensive everything was in New York, was that big cities were horrible. The buildings closed you in, the crowds pushed you down. The day was choked with smog and the night was shut off from the stars. Her great-grandparents had climbed aboard trains heading west the first chance they could. Elizabeth would be lucky to go to the University of Idaho.

She spent a year there, taking geography and history classes, memorizing the details of places that were too far away in miles or too far back in time to travel to. She met a saxophonist named Hollis who wanted to play in clubs. He had a little money and thought they could go to Chicago, but Elizabeth convinced him it had to be New York. After her last final exam, she packed up her suitcases and sold her beat-up Ford. On the bus heading east she wrote a letter to her parents, breaking the news as gently as she could. She told them she and Hollis were planning to get married. But they didn't marry. They lived far out in Brooklyn, and Elizabeth rode the subway over an hour each way to attend City College. She got a job as a waitress, while Hollis smoked and drank and played music in the street. A year before I was born, when my mother was twenty-one, she was finishing her degree in accounting with a minor in history and working five nights a week, hoping that Hollis would start getting gigs that were paid in more than beer. She worked late at the diner, but he was out later than she was. They didn't explore New York together the way they used to, trying out whatever food was foreign and cheap and could be eaten while walking, making fun of stores and hairdos, stopping in parks to kiss on benches.

And then one day a musician friend told her that Hollis had been seen dancing with a slutty jazz singer, dancing too late at night and too often and too close. Elizabeth was furious, but before she confronted Hollis for this and other sins, she went out and had her own affair. A man several years older than she was came into the diner to drink coffee and flirt. Now she flirted back in earnest. By the time she found out she was pregnant, she and Hollis had split up, and she was back in Idaho, visiting her parents, who'd never liked him anyway. They missed their daughter who had, after all, not done so badly. She'd graduated from college with honors and a B.A. in accounting, and she hadn't been mugged or raped or murdered or had the country glow knocked out of her. She was flushed and docile. She walked in the fields in the early morning, nauseated, amid the moaning of the cows. If she stayed with her parents, they would take care of her in their quietly efficient, only slightly disapproving way. She decided to return to New York to struggle on her own. Had she, too, found herself in an abortion clinic, only to walk away still pregnant? In the end, it seemed, she was determined to follow through with me, as she had been determined to make it in New York, to support herself, to make practical plans for the future, and to leave a cheating man—though not as the innocent wounded party, but guilty herself.

She got a job at an accounting firm and worked until they let her go on maternity leave. As for the diner customer, she never saw him again. But she was sure that he, and not Hollis, was my father, and she was glad of it. If I had been Hollis's child, she would probably have broken down and told him, which would have meant that her life would be forever entwined with his. One of the many beauties of New York City, a beauty shaded with disappointment and resentment, was that you could stay in it for the rest of your life, avoiding your past, living another life than the one you thought you were going to live.

What had never occurred to me until I was pregnant

with a potential child I hadn't planned to have, and by a man I didn't expect to see ever again, was that my mother might have kept me for the company. Though of course she didn't know this at the time, she would never have another serious relationship. There were men who drifted in and out, whom she tried to manage along with the daughter she was raising herself, and her demanding job, and going back to Idaho when she could to care for her ailing and then dying parents. If she hadn't had me, who knows what other company might have come along? And what if I hadn't demanded ballet lessons from the age of six on up; and if she had been able to pursue her love of geography and history instead of plugging away at people's taxes for reliable pay; and if her boss hadn't insisted she attend a training in Atlanta that she never got to, because a taxi driver made the worst possible mistake? I was always aware of the sacrifices my mother made for me, and in a number of little ways she didn't fail to remind me of those sacrifices. But to dwell on that was to tumble toward one of those tunnels into which I'd barred the entrance.

It was getting late, and Anne was expected at her in-laws'. Elaine was heading home to Nancy; they were in the middle of watching a TV series I'd never heard of on Netflix. Lara could look forward to a chat with any number of online guys. We settled the bill and went out into lovely May. It was hard to be in the light. Down the street a middle-aged woman pushed an older woman in a wheelchair. The older woman wore a corsage and her head was cocked to one side as if someone was speaking very strongly to her in that ear. The four of us hugged or kissed each other goodbye.

"We should see each other more often."

"Yes, let's do that."

"You're going this way, right?" Lara gestured toward our subway line.

"Actually, Karyn, could you walk with me a minute?" Anne's hand was firm on my shoulder.

"Sure," I said, surprised.

Lara looked surprised too, but she said, "Well, take care, dears," and crossed the street.

"I should pick up some flowers. I think there's a place down here," Anne said. We turned away from the pub. A sign in the drugstore on the corner read "Remember Your Mother. Chocolate Hearts!"

"I remember her. I remember that she didn't like chocolate," Anne said.

"Really?"

"If someone gave her a box of chocolates, she'd break off the shell and just eat the cream inside."

"My mom hated olives, so when I was little I thought I didn't like them either. In third grade a kid at school offered me one, and I told him my mom didn't eat them. 'So?' he said. 'So?' I realized the flaw in my logic, and I ate an olive. I couldn't believe how good it was."

We walked past a gaggle of parents and young children. Everyone, even the dads, was dressed in pastel.

"If this adoption thing works out, I guess my daughter will realize early on how different she is from me," Anne said. "I guess that's a good thing."

"It's really exciting," I said. I waited nervously for her to offer more, to explain why she'd wanted me to walk with her.

"Oh, there's the store," Anne said. The bodega sold flowers under an awning outside. A few bouquets of roses remained, on sale, along with bouquets of their poorer cousin, the carnation.

"I just don't think they're a beautiful flower," I said, pointing to the carnations.

"Yeah, they look raggedy. The roses are so tightly wound, and the carnations are just kind of splayed out there, trying but not making it." We laughed, and I realized that any disapproval I'd felt toward Anne had been replaced by admiration. She put her hand on my shoulder again.

"How are you doing?"

"I'm, well, I'm okay."

"You seemed to be mulling something over this afternoon."

I hesitated, leaning into the lilacs. What did she know, or think that she knew? Sometimes my mother had seemed fully absorbed in her own concerns, and then she'd come out with an observation about me that I couldn't deny, though I tried to, with the vehemence of a young person convinced that to be known by a parent, even in one's graces and triumphs, was fundamentally an embarrassment. If my mother were here today would I persist in that evasion, or would I lay my sorrows and my tiny burst of joy at her feet?

"I feel weird telling you this."

"I'm a social worker, remember? Weird is what I know."

"Okay. I'm pregnant. Thirteen weeks. The guy is gone, but I'm going to have the baby." The colors of the flowers were kaleidoscoping in my eyes. I wiped my nose with the back of my hand. A noise escaped my throat, like the squeak of a hinge. I couldn't look at Anne.

"What do you think of the irises?" she asked. "They don't last very long, but you can't beat that blue."

"Pretty," I managed.

"There's a bench down the street," Anne said. "Why don't I finish up here and I'll see you there in a minute."

I stumbled over to the bench. It was next to the kind of tree that is carefully doled out on well-tended New York City blocks, a tree with its own tiny plot of dirt, fenced off protectively and given its best chance to grow. Anne was coming toward me with two bouquets of flowers, irises and lilacs, wrapped up in paper cones. She smiled with the pride of a woman bearing something beautiful. She set her canvas bag down on the bench and gently angled the irises inside it.

"These are for me, though when my mother-in-law sees them, she'll think they're for her." The dizzying scent of the lilacs enveloped me. Anne placed them in my hands.

"And these are for you."

Tanglewood

Until her sophomore year in college, Elise had thought the term was *unrequieted love.* Love that would not be quiet, would not shut up, though it should, because what was the use of shouting at a deaf person? Then an English professor circled the offending word in her paper on Proust. Mortified by the error—someone who wanted to be a writer shouldn't make such a mistake—Elise looked up the etymology of the word. *Un*—not; *requite*—to pay up. Yes, that was right. Unrequited love did not pay up. You spent everything you had, and what did you get in return? Once, she'd plucked a quarter from the dirty-clothes-strewn carpet of Sam's dorm room, and with a heartbreaking grin he'd said, "Keep it." And yet, Elise had to agree with Nietzsche, whom she'd read in the existentialism class where she and Sam had met, first semester of their sophomore year. "Indispensable . . . to the lover is his unrequited love, which he would at no price relinquish for a state of indifference." Kierkegaard was also profound on the subject, with his depiction of two knights in love with an unattainable princess. The Knight of Infinite Resignation is forever resigned to his inability to realize his one great love. The Knight of Faith believes, despite all evidence to the contrary, that he will win her in the end.

Elise spent the rest of college in kinship with Nietzsche and Kierkegaard, and then, the summer after graduation, she wrote Sam a letter, filled with extravagant metaphors and wild hope. A month later, he sent a two-sentence reply on a torn-out sheet from a yellow legal pad. *I value your friendship, but I cannot return your feelings. I respect and admire you, but I'm not in love with you.* The coldness of the thing was a kind of cure. Elise clipped it to the last page of a diary filled with swoons and laments, as punishment for all the mawkish writing she'd allowed herself to do. Every time she started to long for Sam, she pictured the words in that letter, black on yellow.

Thirteen summers later, Elise had a husband; a sizeable bump due to be born in three months; and a newly published book of poetry, containing no poems about her unrequited first love, Sam. She'd met Derek four years earlier in San Francisco, when she was getting her MFA and Derek was doing a postdoc in chemistry. It was the first time a relationship felt equal to her, not one person wishing or angling for more than the other, not the pining nor the pulling back, but the strangely kinetic feeling of moving forward together, like two people rowing a two-person boat. They got married, moved to the D.C. area for Derek's job, discussed how many children to have.

After a few months of sex off the pill, Elise felt a tingling in her breasts, a queasiness down her throat. Derek took a picture of the plus sign on the test stick. They started mentally rearranging the furniture, debating names, looking at baby gear online. Four weeks later, Elise began to bleed. She'd been observing herself in the mirror with interest, as if she were a woman containing a feminine secret rather than a woman who didn't quite look young anymore—and then she was herself again.

Miscarriage had always struck her as an ugly, unapproachable word, but now Elise appreciated its odd formality. She consulted the *Webster's* she kept on her desk. The first definition was "failure to carry out what was intended [a *miscarriage* of justice]"; the second, "failure of mail, freight, etc. to reach its destination"; the third, "the natural expulsion of an embryo or fetus from the womb before it is sufficiently developed to survive." The order of this list was somehow comforting: the primacy of thwarted justice, of wayward mail, over the loss of a pregnancy.

Three months later, she was pregnant again. This time the plus sign went undocumented. They didn't stay up late, discussing the future life of an embryo smaller than the head of a pin. Things seemed as likely to go wrong as to go right. It wasn't until the midwife showed them the fetus on the ultrasound at eleven weeks that Elise began to believe a baby might very well come of this. But even then, she kept thinking of that old-fashioned word, *expecting*. To be expecting was to assume that something would happen— but one could be wrong, one could be disillusioned, one could live in a permanent state of unfulfilled hope.

When her poetry book was published, Elise lined up as many readings as she could and traveled around the country at her own expense, losing money on her book, as poets did. She wanted to invest as much effort on its behalf as she could while the book was new, and before the baby was born. A Facebook friend who'd once lived in the Berkshires recommended a charming bookstore in a charming town, and so Elise set up a reading there. She hadn't been in touch with Sam since he'd sent the letter that destroyed her hopes, but from Googling him occasionally, she knew he taught music at a public high school in that very town. She hadn't intended to never speak to Sam again—she valued their friendship, too—but after his rejection, she hadn't wanted to connect again until her circumstances had changed and she was no longer the tentative girl pining for a future she wasn't sure she deserved.

Now that she was thirty-four, she could recognize that at twenty-one she'd been, if not beautiful, pretty enough, certainly worthy of someone's desire. Frown lines and crow's feet had emerged in her face now; under her clothes, her skin was coarser and her body more flaccid than it used to be (though she was still young, of course she was; it was obnoxious to complain of being old when you were in your thirties). But the sapphire ring on her finger, the purposeful bulge at her midsection—this was evidence that she was wanted, that she contained multitudes, or at least one miraculous new life. Elise rubbed her hand over her stomach, her own genie in a bottle. She was probably more satisfied with herself now than she had ever been—and she might never be this satisfied again.

She decided to email Sam, keeping it casual (*Hey, old college buddy*), letting him know that she'd be coming his way. Sam emailed back promptly: *Wonderful to hear from you! Congratulations on the book—I knew you'd do it someday.* His guest room was available, he wrote, if she needed a place to stay while she was in town. Just like that they were back in touch, and she was going to see him again, as a woman married to a man she loved, a woman well-published and well-pregnant.

There was still a good ways left to drive, but as soon as Elise saw a sign welcoming her to the Berkshires, she thought of it all as belonging to him. Sam of the long eyelashes and curly brown hair. Sam of the sporadic zit, the floppy old-man hat, the good-luck necklace of baby teeth his mother had made for him. Sam, who could do everything, or everything that mattered. He played piano, clarinet, and saxophone. He sang and acted in college theater productions. He drew fantastic pictures in a sketchbook. One night when they were studying together in his dorm room, Sam sitting at his desk, Elise cross-legged on his bed, he kept looking up at her. She bored her eyes into *Middlemarch,* felt the heat in her cheeks. Could this finally be it? The moment he would come over and take her hands and then make love to her, and when it hurt, because she was a virgin, crack a gentle joke that would allow her to relax and enjoy it? At the end of a long, dense page she'd read several times, she raised her eyes to meet Sam's. He had his sketchbook in his lap, draped over his biology textbook.

"Keep your head down," he said, pen grazing the paper. "Nice eyebrows."

When he was finished, he ripped the page out and gave it to her. *Elise, Reading,* he'd written at the top. In the bottom right corner, he'd signed his name. It was her, she had to admit it—the squarish face, the bumpy nose, the heavy eyebrows. Nothing to do but praise his work, hide her disappointment. She still had the picture, folded once, right through her mouth, tucked into that annotated Penguin edition of *Middlemarch.* That was Sam: her study partner; her cafeteria-table seatmate; her Friday night, don't-have-a-date, movie companion; but never her boyfriend, never her lover.

Elise was off the highway now, the Berkshires in early June parading before her. She passed fields dotted with cows; clapboard houses skirted by rose gardens; whole families on bicycles; elderly couples on porch swings; railroad tracks; main streets with post offices, art galleries, cheese and ice cream shops. From time to time, the Housatonic River appeared, flanked with trees, a postcard of lovely and placid New England.

The summer after junior year, when they'd both lived in New York, working office jobs, Elise and Sam had boarded a Port Authority bus together one weekend, bound for the Berkshires. Sam and his bassist friend Clint had bought tickets to see the Boston Symphony at Tanglewood, and then Clint's grandfather had died, and he couldn't go. Elise was the substitute. All those hours sitting beside each other on a bus—what had they talked about? Sam would have told her things about the repertoire at the concert they were going to attend. He would have shared his headphones, his cassette tapes of symphonies copied from the library, instructing her on how to listen for the themes and variations, the sonic elements she could really only hear if they were pointed out to her; otherwise, the music just became a winding river, with nothing detectable beneath the dark, glistening surface. They would have discussed how they were spending their days, the minutiae of their boring jobs, and the weird people who worked in those offices, and the tiny anecdotes of life in New York, saved up for a like-minded person to laugh at. For some time they would have sat in silence, looking out the window, and Elise would have monitored the force field between their elbows and their knees; she would have been wearing something soft, softer than anything she owned now.

The lawn at Tanglewood shone green-green-green, with picnic blankets and lemonade and the Taconic Mountains in the distance. The concert hall glimmered gold as the heart of fire: polished wood of cellos, flinty nickel of flutes, the sounds struck by almost a hundred instruments vibrating with air. Then the room they shared at the B&B, with its high double beds, quilts glowing pure white in the half-moonlight, while Elise lay awake, thinking that anything, failure and humiliation, would be better than the forever regret of not doing it, not climbing into the bed two feet away from her own, where Sam's cheek grazed the pillow; where his body could only be warm under blankets on a summer night; where he would have to concede, whatever his reservations about her, that skin wanted to touch skin—and not doing it. Instead, sinking down into the leadenness of time passing no matter what, and then waking up to running water in the bathroom and Sam coming out fully dressed, combing his wet hair, saying, "Let's go downstairs and see how much we can eat for breakfast."

Sam's street was lined with oak trees and Cape Cod–style houses painted steel gray, forest green, sailor-suit blue. His front yard was bordered with ragged peonies. Elise wondered if Sam had planted them himself, or if they'd been growing here before he bought the house. The kind of detail it used to seem vital to know: the lover's imperative, the poet's imperative, to collect, collect—as if scraps of information were a kind of currency, as if you could save them up to buy something you'd never thought you could afford. He opened the door and gave her a hug, then stepped back and looked at her belly.

"Well. I don't want to presume."

"I'm pregnant."

"Phew." He smiled with his same face, older but the same. Crinkles around his brown eyes, his thinning hair a bit scraggly, the worn-out T-shirt and jeans of a guy who didn't give a damn about clothes. Even back then he wasn't the kind of person you'd fall in love with at first sight. It had taken a whole semester of sitting next to him in that existentialism class, in those uncomfortable lecture hall seats, watching him doodle extravagant monsters and bearded philosophers in his notes, exchanging a few playful words after class, before she could admit to herself that she'd never wanted anyone as much as she wanted him.

He took her around the house and she admired all the rooms with their rag rugs, woven baskets, antique toys, sheer white curtains. *A woman's touch*—dumb phrase—kept running through her head. But no, he must live here alone. He would have told her otherwise. And it all seemed like Sam's good taste, his deliberate artistic handiwork. He didn't care how he looked, and he could be messy, but he'd managed to class up a college dorm room with a pretty red lampshade, a lush plant, incense burning in a wooden holder carved like a tiger.

The refrigerator was decorated with pictures of two adorable children. "My niece and nephew," Sam said, pouring her a glass of iced tea. "They call me Uncle Sam. Actually, Meg's coming to your reading tonight."

"She is?"

"They live just a few towns over. Her husband will stay home with the kids. Since I'm assuming your poems aren't about dogs and cats and pizza."

Elise had met Sam's sister a few times. Four years older than them, she'd been working in Boston as a consultant: a sexy, adult job. Meg looked like Sam—cute, not remarkable—but she'd made herself hot by wearing funky, revealing clothes, and joking about sex with just the right amount of knowing self-deprecation. Elise was uncomfortable around Meg, sure that Sam's sister was wise to her painful crush. If Meg had had such a crush, she would have gotten drunk and taken care of it one way or another, rather than waiting around for years, stupidly hoping, and finally writing a letter, the coward's way out.

Elise asked about Sam's teaching and his music, and he told her that after living in New York for six years after college, trying to get gigs and giving private lessons, he got tired of just scraping by and did a master's in music education, then applied for the high school job here because he thought it would be nice to live close to Meg and her family. "So I'm not as cool as I thought I was, but I like my teenage minions. And I play with a quartet. We get down to New York sometimes. In the summer there's a music scene around here, with Tanglewood nearby. Have you ever been out for it?"

"Not since—not in a long time."

Elise forced down a gulp of tea. Did he really not remember that weekend? Just the word *Tanglewood* and she was back in that ghostly bedroom, with the night draining away the thought that she might be brave enough to disturb the universe.

"That's right, we took the bus up," Sam said, as if she'd reminded him. "They did the Mendelssohn violin concerto and Prokofiev, the 'Lieutenant Kijé' suite." He hummed a bit of something that sounded familiar. Sam could slip into a tune as easily as a jacket, and he would hum it just long enough to suggest that singing was superior to speech. "Too bad the season doesn't start till next month."

He gestured toward her belly. "So tell me—boy or girl? Do you know?"

"We decided to go the old-fashioned route and be surprised."

"I think I'd do that too. Prolong the mystery."

One night when they were eating together in the dining hall, Sam had talked about wanting to have kids someday. "I'd be a good father, don't you think?" he said, puffing out his chest. She did, she did. But she'd just laughed and left the table to get a dish of vanilla soft serve, trying not to start mulling over what they would name their babies. Now she thought about asking Sam if he still wanted kids. But she didn't want to hear him say that he did, he just hadn't found the right woman yet. He was a man; he had plenty of time. When they first got to be friends, she'd wondered if he might be gay. Maybe that was why he was so damn good at the arts, so sensitive to beautiful things. Was that why they could walk around campus talking, laughing, never holding hands? But no. As it turned out, there had been girls; there would be women. Sam just didn't discuss them. So she was free to fantasize that their future together was inevitable; it didn't mean he wasn't interested just because they hadn't become a couple yet.

"Are you feeling it move a lot?" Sam asked. "It. The creature."

"The alien."

"Do you feel like you've been colonized?"

"It's funny, being on this book tour—such as it is—I feel like I'm traveling with someone else. A perpetual audience. But I have no idea who this audience member is."

"Right, like does it enjoy your poetry, or is it secretly thinking, 'Lady, I don't know what you're talking about.'"

Elise laughed. She'd always basked in Sam's teasing, welcomed it as a kind of intimacy.

"So you're going to give birth to this little critic. Are you excited? Terrified?"

His face shone with that intense curiosity, that genuine interest, that she'd found so desirable.

"Both, I guess. I keep telling myself to think about it, to prepare somehow, but I can't get my mind around what it's going to be like."

If Elise were less on guard, less determined to present herself to Sam as flourishing (while being disarmingly humble about her successes, of course), she might have told him about the miscarriage, how it had made her alert to the precariousness of it all. Developing organs could quit growing. A beating heart could just stop. During delivery, a few minutes of insufficient oxygen could mean a lifetime of damage. A bacterial infection could attack a tiny body—born and then gone. But no, he had lost the privilege to be close to her, to know her desires and her fears. She'd wanted to bare all of that to him, and she'd been afraid to, and with a few sentences dispatched through the mail, he'd wiped out her vision of what could be. And now she was standing in his kitchen, a visibly pregnant woman, the way pregnant women stood as if on display, as if embodying love and life and hope for the future—all of the things that others, and the women themselves, wanted to see.

Elise was the last poet to read, after two fifty-something women, Berkshire locals. She heard herself being gracious, thanking the bookstore owner who'd invited her to come, the audience of twenty or so people, no doubt most of them friends of the other poets. She began to read the Post-it Note–marked poems in her book. When she'd started writing, she was all about yearning and despair. Writing poems about Sam was her weakness. They were bad and she knew it. But there was something consoling in trying to put her feelings into a poem and failing. Sam couldn't overtake the page; there was no monument erected to his greatness. One day, she thought, she'd transcend the who-cares-about-your-dumb-love-life poems and capture the aching perfection of the exquisite swoon: love as disaster, love as elixir, love as crushing flood and holy water. It hadn't happened yet. Instead, she had started writing about other things: the origins of words, geological structures, weather patterns, household objects. She'd made a book out of intriguing distractions and chiseled restraint. She read her last poem, thanked everyone again, and allowed herself one glance at Sam. He was clapping vigorously, his face flushed and smiling. She knew that look from years ago, from the dorm room, when he would turn around to take a break from studying, and she would say something that pleased him, that seemed to slip inside his skin and switch on a light. It was that look of pleasure that had given her the most hope.

As the small audience dispersed, a woman, young and pretty, tapped Sam on the shoulder, and Elise was struck by a jealous twinge. Then Meg put an arm around her shoulders and steered her toward the table by the cash register, where the poets would sign books. "That was awesome," Meg said. "I was afraid I might have to lie to you afterward."

Elise laughed. "How do I know you're not lying right now?"

"I can't even lie to my kids. Really, you were good."

"Thanks. It's great to see you again."

"I always liked you. You were mysterious."

"You mean I was shy."

"In a good way. I approved."

"You approved?"

"For a while I thought you and Sam were together, and he just wasn't telling me."

"Oh." Elise's hand went to her belly, a protective gesture—for herself, not her womb.

Meg leaned in. "I think he made a mistake," she said. "But anyway, you're doing great. You got a book published. You're married. You're having a baby."

She'd pinpointed the reasons that made it seem okay to see Sam again, but it was disconcerting to hear them directly articulated. Like Elise was trying too hard, still, to get Sam to notice her. What could she say to his sister? She didn't have to say anything. One of the other readers was coming toward her, waving Elise's book and a pen.

She sat on Sam's couch, drinking a mojito minus the rum. The stereo was playing Debussy, one of Sam's favorites, oboes and flutes chasing each other like nymphs through a forest. After she'd signed a few books at the bookstore, they'd gone out for Japanese food with Meg and that woman who'd been talking to Sam, an English teacher at the high school, who, Elise had learned with an irritating flicker of relief, had a boyfriend at home. And now she and Sam were alone at his house. He was sitting in a rocking chair with his sleepy eyes fixed on her, his chin resting on his hands. "Thirteen years since we graduated, huh? When you look back on college, are you nostalgic?"

Fuck you—you were college, she thought. "Are you?" she replied.

"I asked you first."

"Sure, I'm nostalgic. To get to take classes and read books all the time. To be young and in school, with my parents footing the bill. Of course I didn't appreciate it enough at the time."

Sam took a long sip of his properly alcohol-laden mojito, and Elise wished she could have a couple of strong drinks. It had taken until her mid-twenties, but she had finally learned how to make use of the emboldening properties of alcohol. Now she had to pretend her sticky-sweet drink was bitter with the stuff. She didn't want to keep sitting with him the way she used to, not expressing what she was thinking so strongly that it seemed like he had to know it. But she was old enough now to recognize that wasn't how things worked. People were their own individual planets, spinning in their own orbits, and to reach someone else you had to throw a meteor sometimes.

"That letter I sent, after we graduated. It was pretty embarrassing."

"Nah, it was poetry."

"I don't think so."

Sam took another long sip. "Well, I want to apologize," he said. "The letter I sent you was pretty lame."

"Yeah, it was."

"You deserved better. But I didn't think it would mean we wouldn't speak again for thirteen years."

"Did you tell Meg about it?"

"Uh, yeah. Just last week. She wanted to know why we were out of touch for so long."

Elise was tempted to tell him what Meg had said about his making a mistake. But she could only fling her meteor so far.

"Look, can I ask you something?" Sam said. "What was it that made you feel, you know, the way you did then?"

He'd stolen her question and flipped it—the question she was afraid to ask, that she didn't know how to ask in a way that didn't seem whiny or pathetic, but merely curious, a philosopher seeking knowledge: *Why didn't you love me?*

She wanted to throw her virgin cocktail in his face,

though really he had done nothing wrong. She was the one who had brought the matter up, who couldn't simply go back to being friends and keep that unrequited business quiet. So she blundered through a vague answer, what anyone might say about loving anyone—the way we talked, the way we laughed, the things we did together, just a feeling.

"Well hey, I'm glad you broke the silence," he said, when she was done with her fumbling. "It's good to see you again."

He was as maddening as he'd always been—laying the groundwork for intimacy, charging the atmosphere with intensity, and then wriggling his way out of it, acting like everything was cool. Derek's vulnerability had been a revelation; he told her he loved her every day. But at the moment, having such a man for her husband didn't feel like enough. She wanted restitution for the past, too.

The wallpaper in the guest room had to have been chosen by a previous resident, some woman of floral tastes. Even a guy fond of classical music and a pretty lampshade wouldn't choose to cover the walls of a room with yellow roses. The worn plaid comforter on the bed seemed familiar, though: the look of it, the feel of it, the smell. It must be the same one that had covered the standard-issue dorm bed where she'd perched while Sam worked at the desk and music sounded from the speakers

on his cheap CD player—a tender piano sonata, a knowing
string quartet—composed more than a hundred years
ago, when the only way you could hear music was to go to
a concert or to make it yourself; music so beautiful that,
listening to it, you felt it must make you beautiful too, must
work like some beneficent cancer, merging with the cells in
your body, changing their structure.

On the bookshelf, Elise recognized some of Sam's old
college texts: *An Introduction to Art History, Civilization and
Its Discontents, A Kierkegaard Anthology.* When she'd moved
to San Francisco for graduate school, she'd donated her
own copy of Kierkegaard to the public library, along with a
slew of other books that had been important to her. She'd
had to force herself to do it, to rise above sentimentality.
She pulled the Kierkegaard off the shelf and leafed through
it till she found the section on the Knight of Infinite
Resignation. Sitting down on the bed, she began to read.
"A young swain falls in love with a princess, and the whole
content of his life consists in this love, and yet the situation
is such that it is impossible for it to be realized, impossible
for it to be translated from ideality into reality. The slaves
of paltriness, the frogs in life's swamp, will naturally cry
out, 'Such a love is foolishness. The rich brewer's widow is a
match fully as good and respectable.' Let them croak in the
swamp undisturbed. It is not so with the knight of infinite
resignation: he does not give up his love, not for all the
glory of the world."

Sam had underlined various passages, drawn asterisks in

the margins. She'd found this piece so gorgeous. Sam, she thought, had found it so too. He just hadn't been thinking of her when he read it.

She thought about calling Derek, but she was back in the time before him now. The time when love was not about living with someone, and making decisions together, and pledging yourselves to a future child you'd created, but about lying in a single bed and longing for someone you only touched when you were side by side in a lecture hall or on a bus, and your elbow brushed his, and the sensual thrill was so great you couldn't bear to get up when the class or the bus ride ended. She had told Derek that she was going to stay with an old college friend, but she hadn't told him about the feelings she'd had for Sam. He was not a jealous sort, and he trusted her, but what would be the point of turning the story of her love into an anecdote, a childish thing to laugh at or wave away?

She sent Derek a text: *Reading went well. Super tired— xoxo,* and then got under the covers and rolled onto her side. In a moment, the baby began to move. These jolts had been happening for over a month, but she hadn't really gotten used to them. Just a few tough layers of skin, a few pounds' worth of uterus and placenta, separating her from this unknown being that would become—that would have to become—a monumental force in her life forever. In a year this baby would be crawling, scooping up everything it could get its hands on, shoving coins carelessly dropped on the carpet into its mouth. In twenty years this baby would be in college, racking up a lifetime's worth of nostalgia. In forty years it could be lugging around its own disappointments and regrets and sense of time already running out, and she herself would be an old woman or dead.

In the middle of the night she woke up, as she always did lately, her bladder about to burst. She went out to the bathroom in the hall, flushed the toilet, ran the water in the sink, turned off the light, and paused there between her room and Sam's. His door was halfway open, the outline of his ornate bureau visible in the dark. It was three a.m. logic, but she felt as if she could walk into his room and get into bed—that she had that right. She stepped closer to his door. Now she could see the shape of him, the sheet pulled up over his body, the back of his neck exposed, between his white T-shirt and his dark hair. After all this time, it wasn't even that she really wanted to. She loved being in bed with Derek, his familiar warm skin, the way they ran their hands over each other and talked and had sex, as if it was all one thing, one conjoined life. What she wanted at this moment was something impossible, to be in that July night fourteen years in the past, when she might have been bold enough to slide into the borrowed bed with the young man she'd wanted to be her first lover, her first relationship. The two of them just twenty years old, the orchestra at Tanglewood still playing in their heads.

Suddenly Sam's eyes were open and he was looking at her. "You okay?" he asked.

"Oh yeah, just had to go to the bathroom."

He lifted his head up, off the pillow. She could walk in

there and lie down, press her big, solid belly against him, and perhaps he wouldn't protest, having learned by now that a night like this wouldn't have to change anything. What would it feel like? Compensation, triumph, disaster?

"Go back to sleep," Elise said. "See you in the morning."

He sank his head back on the pillow.

She turned toward the rose-wallpapered guest room and got under Sam's old comforter, that familiar swell rising up, of loneliness and yearning. The Kierkegaard tome sat, stately, on the nightstand. And she began to narrate the story to herself.

A young poet fell in love with a young musician, who didn't return her sentiments. For a time, he was the glory of her world. Life went on—the frogs croaked in the swamp undisturbed. Then, years later, she gave up her love. The woman is no fool.

June

As the baby was growing inside Natalie's uterus, her aunt
Dina was dying. It became an awful race: which would
happen first, the birth or the death? If the baby came
first, that meant Dina could see her, the new life dandled
before the one on the way out. Natalie's mother expressed
a tearful hope that Dina would hold on long enough to
meet her grandniece. Natalie secretly preferred the death
to come first, not so it could be followed by a joyous event,
but because she didn't want the baby to detract from it.
She wasn't a practicing Jew, but she wanted to mourn in the
traditional Jewish way: stop everything, tear her clothes,
sit around all day for a week with relatives she didn't much
like, and accept plates of heavy food she didn't want to eat.
With the congratulatory emails, and the round-the-clock
nursing, and the adorable outfits, how could a newborn fit
into that ritual of grief?

Up late with nausea and worry, Natalie considered these
two lives—Dina's and the baby's. Which one would she
choose? She had played games like this as an only child in

the backseat on long car rides. If just one could be saved—
the dog or the cat, her gymnastics team or her Hebrew
School class, her mom or her dad—which would it be?
While her parents talked to each other about work and
bills and other people's problems, she silently deliberated.
By the time they got to Providence, or Cape May, or the
Finger Lakes, she had to decide. The dog, the gymnastics
team, her dad, Dina.

Dina's son, Matt, had been born on March twenty-
first, Natalie's half birthday. She was six-and-a-
half that year. It was a strange and fascinating fact that
on September twenty-first, when she would forever be
turning another year older, Matt would forever be having
his half birthday. Maybe, Natalie thought, Matt was a
kind of half twin. A woman at the supermarket had once
asked, wasn't she lonely with no brothers or sisters, and
Natalie supposed that she was. She made her new cousin
a card with a joke in it. "WELCOME MATT," it said, with
a picture of a baby boy lying on a red rug in front of a
door. She helped her mom pick out a onesie and a stuffed
monkey and wrap them in polka-dotted paper. She ran up
Aunt Dina and Uncle Rob's driveway with the card and
package in her hand. Dina opened the door, wearing a gray
nightgown, her black hair wild around her face. The baby
was hiding in a blanket against her chest, and Natalie felt
suddenly shy.

"Isn't he funny-looking?" Dina asked, tilting the bundle in her arms so that Natalie could see.

"Yes," she said.

"He's precious," her mom protested. But Matt looked more like a shrunken Charlie Brown than a half twin.

In the living room, Dina asked Natalie if she wanted to hold him.

"Oh, not yet. He's so tiny," Natalie's mom said.

"She can handle it," Dina said. "What do you think, Natalie?"

"I'll sit on the floor so I don't drop him."

"Good idea," Dina said.

Natalie made a nest with her lap and Dina lowered the baby into it. When Matt began to fuss, Natalie put her finger up to his mouth. Matt sucked on her nail, his weird, no-color eyes crossing.

"You know just what to do," Dina said. "You'll be like a big sister to him. You'll be better than a big sister."

Later, when the three of them were lying in Dina's bed, her aunt asked Natalie: "Will you help me take care of him? I need all the help I can get."

Natalie didn't like helping out at home: clearing the table, sorting the laundry, keeping her room clean. But this was different. Her aunt hadn't pleaded, bribed, nagged, or demanded, the way her mom did. She had asked. Of course Natalie would help. She fetched baby bottles, retrieved dropped toys, pushed swings, wrestled on jackets and shoes, soothed hurts. She and Dina sat on the bench under the trees at the playground and talked, while Matt ran around and shouted and flung sand out of the sandbox.

Matt was twenty-four now, living in Manhattan and working as a production assistant at an independent film company. Natalie worked at a law firm in Midtown; she took her cousin out for lunch sometimes. Though she and Matt were technically of the same generation, Natalie still felt maternal toward him. She was Dina's friend first, then Matt's cousin. It had always been that way. She had become a lawyer, like Dina, and had moved back to Connecticut, near both Dina and her parents.

When Natalie was Matt's age, it had seemed lame to work in the city and live outside of it. Why spend your free hours in the suburbs when the city itself was freedom? But her husband Ian didn't love it the way she did. He'd gone to work for his dad's business in Stamford, and so they'd bought a house close to his office rather than continue renting in New York. At least they were saving money, and had more space, and she could have a pot of green tea with Dina whenever she wanted to.

Now that Ian was comfortably stationed on a street where the trees formed a canopy overhead, and the neighbors were tucked away inside their stone and brick mini-fortresses, the city was hers again, if only in a piecemeal way. She had the twelve-block walk to and from the train station to her office. She had the view of the Chrysler Building and Bryant Park from the conference room window. She had her lunch hour. She had the occasional night out with friends after work. The commute was its own daily pleasure—the train zipping by all the little anonymous scenes, the splendid portal of Grand Central Terminal awaiting her. Gazing up at the luminous light-green ceiling with its gold-etched constellations was a kind of worship, even better than looking at a brilliant sky, because it was a manmade beauty, a triumph of human achievement.

Just after Labor Day, Natalie had stood in Grand Central and answered a call from her mother. It was six o'clock and the high windows still pitched out bands of light. With the train not due to leave for fourteen minutes, she was in the serene position of watching others scurry.

"You're on your way home?" It sounded like her mother was trying not to cry.

"I have a few minutes. What's going on?"

"I can't. Not on the phone. Come by later."

"Tell me. I'll worry all the way home."

"You should worry."

It wasn't what Natalie's mind had leapt to: something had happened with her dad's job, to her grandfather in the nursing home. It was worse than that. Dina, stomach cancer, stage 4.

With its columns and arches, its marble floors and domed ceiling, Grand Central Terminal had a way of drawing everything into itself. Standing there, surrounded by so many sources of light—windows, wall sconces, chandeliers, display boards, illuminated clocks—you could pretend that grandeur was all. Forget your obligations to other people. Forget the mind's tedious habits. Forget the body. Forget time. Except that time was master here; you couldn't outwit it. Natalie's train would depart in thirteen minutes, and even if she willfully missed it, another train would arrive thirty-seven minutes after that, and another an hour after that, and then another one, all going to the same place.

Two pink lines you were pregnant; one pink line you weren't. The instructions didn't say how to interpret a second line so faint it barely seemed to constitute a line at all. Unlike the bathroom in their old New York apartment, this Connecticut bathroom provided plenty of room for two people to deliberate before the sink.

"I'm not really sure that counts as a line," Natalie said.

"I think it counts," Ian said. He was beaming, and she could hardly look at him. They'd been vaguely trying for this for a little while, but in the new rawness of Dina's diagnosis, the glimmer of another life felt almost like a slap in the face to Natalie.

He took her hand and led her to the living room. It was an October evening, the hour between the sunset and the glow of the street lamps. The brown microsuede couch faced the show-off trees. Ian stroked her bare feet in his lap. "So the baby would come in June. That's a great birthday month. The end of school, the beginning of summer."

"It's just such a bad time right now," Natalie said. The

foot-stroking felt good, and nothing should feel good when Dina was as sick as she was.

"It's never the perfect time. That's what everyone says."

"You mean it's always something: a new job, a leaky roof, a little cancer in the family."

The foot-stroking stopped. "But this is a happy thing. Don't you think everyone would be happy for us?"

"Sure they would."

"Then let's celebrate for a minute at least."

Ian had this hunter-green terry-cloth bathrobe that a dad would wear. He liked to speak in funny voices and coach people through their problems. Natalie wanted to have a child with him. But she couldn't focus her energy on that now. She was busy being angry, at the world, at God—even though she didn't believe in God, even though God was just a name in a song, a word in a blessing, a character in a story. Being angry was better than feeling the force of what she was going to lose.

Dina had the tumor removed from her stomach and was now getting treatments (of cell-crushing poison) at a hospital with a fancy Manhattan address. A few blocks away, a gallery displayed four floors of Expressionist masterpieces, a shop sold Turkish rugs, a restaurant served truffles and filet mignon. Dina's condition was too critical to allow her to go home between chemo sessions; she was stuck here. Wednesday was Natalie's regular night. Her mom, Matt, and Dina's two closest friends each had theirs. This way, Dina could count on a dependable retinue of visitors, a network, a rotating team. And this way, they didn't have to see each other: the healthy, ill-at-ease loved ones clustered around the sick one. They could each come to her on their own terms, like Catholics in a confession booth.

Dina's room overlooked an elegant brick building across the street, with gargoyles minding the cornices. When the nurse came to check Dina's vitals, Natalie stood by the window and studied the gargoyles. They were bug-eyed, open-mouthed, hunched over, as if the weight of the building rested on their backs. In medieval times, people thought gargoyles had the power to ward off evil spirits. This seemed like the right idea. Fight ghoulishness with ghoulishness; give fear a suitably fearful shape. Natalie wished the hospital itself were filled with gargoyles rather than with soft-focus paintings of flowers and shorelines, posters printed with inspirational quotes, helpful signage.

December now, holiday time. As she walked down the corridors, Natalie glimpsed wreaths, shiny packages, colorful lights, and cancer patients with all of the meat sucked off their bones. In Dina's room, a tarnished silver menorah teetered on the radiator. It had belonged to her mother. As children, Natalie and Matt always went to their grandmother's crumbling apartment in Washington Heights for the first night of Hanukkah. Their mothers had grown up there, in that cramped apartment with the hissing radiators and peeling paint. Natalie's mom complained about it, tried to get their grandmother to move to a retirement home close to them in Connecticut. "Lay off her," Dina would say. "Her life is here, where the action is. She doesn't want to be with a bunch of old suburbanites."

At the Hanukkah celebration, they ate latkes fried on all four burners of the stove and jelly donuts plucked from a white bakery box. They made their tuneless way through songs about Maccabees and dreidels. They tore open sixteen packages wrapped in *The Jewish Week* and tied with yarn, eight for Natalie and eight for Matt. "Why don't you each open one present now and bring the rest home for the other nights?" Natalie's mother would say.

"No," her grandmother intervened. "Let them do it like the Christians. Everything at once—a big bonanza, so they feel like they're rich."

Her grandmother had been dead fourteen years now, such a long time it wasn't painful to think of her being dead anymore, though Natalie had loved her, and had run away from the family gathering after the funeral, away from her own house, because everyone was just stuffing their faces and talking about stupid things.

Dina was sitting up in the hospital bed, wearing the wig Natalie had helped her pick out. It was nicer than her real hair, which had been scrub-brush coarse and shot through with graying frizz. The silky wig hung in soft waves to Dina's shoulders. "I used to spend a lot of time trying to make my hair look like this," she'd said to Natalie when she tried it on. "It never worked. I guess this is my chance to have the hair I always wanted."

Natalie produced a box of Hanukkah candles from her briefcase and handed it to Dina. "You got the good ones," Dina said. "That sweet Israeli family on the back." A woman with a saintly glow was lighting a giant menorah, while two young boys appeared entranced by their mother's magic. The Western Wall gleamed gold behind them.

Dina opened the box and fingered the wicks. "Do you know why lighting candles is considered a woman's job? Because Eve was responsible for dimming the world's light."

"Goddamn. Maybe we should refuse to light them. Is there some male orderly we can call in?"

"Nope. It's all women on this floor at night. You have to wait until morning for your doctor man to breeze through."

Tonight Natalie was supposed to tell Dina that she was pregnant. The first trimester had passed, and Ian had called his parents, his brother, and his best friends with the news. From the couch, Natalie had listened to him in the kitchen, where he was preparing a healthy, protein-rich meal, as he'd taken it upon himself to do these days. In the reverential tone of the pregnancy magazines in the obstetrician's waiting room, he reported on Natalie's morning sickness, the prenatal tests they had scheduled, their excitement about what was to come.

They told her parents at Sunday brunch, which Natalie

wasn't eating, because omelets smelled like unborn chicks. Her mom squealed, teared up, rushed about fixing Natalie a different breakfast. Her dad hugged them and said he would build the baby a crib.

"Let me tell Dina," Natalie said.

"Of course," her mother said sharply, acting offended at the implication that she had to be instructed to hold her tongue.

Now Natalie lit the *shamash,* the servant candle, which was used to ignite the others, each night lighting one more candle than it had the night before. This was the first night: two flames. "Let's turn out the light," Dina said, and the two of them sat in the almost dark, with the sounds of creaky carts and cheery nurses.

"I want to tell you something but I'm nervous," Natalie said.

"Okay," Dina said.

"It's silly that I'm nervous." Her mom would have said *Don't be.* Dina would not say that.

"I'm pregnant."

"That's wonderful." Dina was looking at her carefully.

"I don't feel that right now," she said. She was embarrassed to be crying, which she hadn't done in front of Dina since her grandmother died. She hadn't cried in her presence this entire fall. The doctors had said that even with aggressive chemo, the odds weren't good. The odds of living, they meant. And here Natalie was, crying over something that was supposed to be wonderful.

"I didn't feel it," Dina said. She pulled a tissue from the

box on her bedside table and handed it to Natalie. "Not till Matt was more than a month old. I felt sick the whole pregnancy. I wanted the baby out of me, but I also wasn't ready. After he was born, the little sleep I got, I had these nightmares. Somehow we'd left him alone in the house. We were neglectful, or maybe we were dead. My son was left completely alone, with no idea what was happening. In the dream I could feel his terror as if it were my own. It was, of course."

Dina's voice was still Dina's voice, thoughtful and calm.

"And I felt resentful, too, and then guilty for feeling that way. You know, in the beginning, there's crying and not crying. There's distressed and there's neutral. I had a really hard time with the lack of positive feedback. I remember when I first felt we had something that might be mutual. Matt was lying in his bassinet, about six weeks old. Suddenly I wanted to sing to him. You know I can't sing. Even 'Happy Birthday'—I move my mouth, but I don't let the sound come out. That day, though, I sang all the songs I can't sing. 'Whole Lotta Love.' 'Very Young.' 'Heart of Gold.' Matt started making this sound: *Oh, oh, oh.* This surprised, amazing sound. He was six weeks old and he liked my singing. I'd been waiting my entire life for someone to want to hear me sing."

It was getting late. Dina had stopped talking, and she looked very tired. But Natalie didn't want to leave until the candles had melted all the way down. One Hanukkah night, years ago, Natalie and her mom had needed to make a semi-emergency trip to the drugstore. As they prepared to leave an empty house behind, the candles in the menorah stood at half their original size, the flames still going strong. Before herding Natalie out the door, her mom blew out the candles. By then, age ten or so, Natalie had already considered the existence of God and found him absent from the heavens, but to extinguish the Hanukkah candles rather than letting them burn down naturally felt like a sacrilege. And yet her mother seemed to do it without a second thought.

Complaining of itchiness, Dina removed the wig. She was completely bald. The muscles in her neck bulged; her face was in retreat. Natalie was relieved to have told Dina about the pregnancy, and, for the first time since she'd learned of it, she was awestruck by what her body was doing. But Dina's body was betraying her at every moment.

Back in high school, Natalie had witnessed another betrayal. It was an ending for Dina—and it coincided with a beginning of sorts for her. One fall day in her sophomore year, when the bell rang at the end of English class, her crush since fifth grade turned around and asked her out. He used to be Billy. Now he went by William. In middle school he'd teased her for getting good grades. Now he wanted to hear her thoughts on *The Odyssey*. She spent the rest of the day in a white heat underneath her clingy sweater. Instead of taking the bus, she walked home from school: an hour's trudge through winding streets with old stone houses and scarlet foliage. Her surroundings registered vaguely as beautiful and boring. She was caught up in a meandering fantasy, though not exactly about her impending date with William. There was excitement in the thought of sitting next to each other in a movie theater, his hand grabbing hers in the dark—but it wasn't the real excitement to come, the excitement that the first date of her life would set into motion. She was imagining being older and living in New York City, gliding down Fifth Avenue on a snowy evening, her long wool coat brushing against the long wool coat of some man, not William, not anyone from Chesterbrook High, no matter how cute he was. They would climb the stairs up to the roof of an apartment building and stand there embracing, pressing all of their heat into each other, while thousands of lights glowing softly in the snow kept promising: more, more, more.

When she arrived home, her mom was on the upstairs phone, shouting about some bastard, some unbelievable bullshit artist. It took Natalie a minute to realize she was talking about Uncle Rob. He'd been having an affair with some woman, cheating on Dina. The kitchen stewed in a mid-dinner-preparation mess: chicken breasts half breaded, boiling potatoes popping out of their red skins, a cutting board full of string beans not yet severed from their pointy ends. Natalie turned off the stove and stood by the sink, sneaking slivered almonds. Was it unbelievable that Rob had turned out to be a bastard and a bullshit artist? He was her uncle, a dentist. He lived a short car ride away, and she had known him all her life. The last time she'd seen him, he asked about her grades, and when she started mumbling about As and A minuses, he boomed, "Excellent, excellent. Keep it up." He had the dentist's requisite glistening smile and the lean physique of a former college tennis player. He was better looking, and more energetic and jovial than Dina, with her serious eyes, her refusal to smile when she didn't feel like smiling. Natalie supposed that most people would consider him the better catch. But Dina was the one who never made small talk, who talked only because she had real things that she wanted to say.

When Natalie's mom finally came downstairs, she went straight to the refrigerator and pulled out a beer.

"I guess you heard," she said, grimacing, as she popped off the top.

"What's Dina going to do?"

"Smart lawyer—she's already had the divorce papers drawn up."

"How did she find out?"

"Oh, these things leave a trail." Natalie wasn't sure if that meant her mom didn't want to disclose the details, or if she wasn't clear on them herself.

"Does Matt know?"

"They'll tell him tomorrow afternoon, poor little boy. What a father. It goes without saying, no New York trip this weekend. You and Daddy and I can go to the movies."

Every other Saturday, some familial combination of Bernsteins and Newbergs took the train to Grand Central. From there they went to a museum, or a show, or a street festival, or just out for Chinese food at Ollie's, followed by a long walk. When William had asked Natalie out for this Saturday, she timidly proposed the following Saturday instead. She could have skipped the family outing, but not without making a bigger deal of this date than she'd felt prepared to do on a day's notice.

"What other questions do you have, honey? I know this is so hard to process."

After the phone tirade, the good mother persona was kicking into gear, that tone of exaggerated concern that never made Natalie want to confess to anything. She wanted to hear about the situation from Dina herself, but she was also afraid to hear it. She had seen her mother hurt many times: crying, bearing a crumpled look that made Natalie ashamed for her, rather than compassionate. Though she'd heard Dina speak harshly at times—to Rob, to Matt, to someone at work who was driving her crazy—it was a kind of controlled anger that seemed warranted, even admirable. Natalie didn't want to find her aunt transformed into a pitiable creature, a cheated-upon wife, whether raging or weeping.

"I'll help you finish making dinner," Natalie said, snapping the ends off the string beans.

On Saturday afternoon she sat between her parents at the local movie theater, watching a documentary about the migratory patterns of birds. It was a compromise. Her mom wanted to see a Holocaust drama. Her dad wanted to see a sci-fi thriller. Natalie wanted to stay home and lie in bed, maybe finish *The Odyssey* reading she had to do. The birds on the screen rose up in flocks, circled the skies, voyaged heroically to distant lands. There weren't any people in this movie, just birds: goofy and elegant, striking and plain. To see them going about their lives was a kind of relief.

The next day Dina called and asked Natalie to come over. Rob had taken Matt out for pizza and bowling. Natalie and her aunt sat on the couch eating pretzels and watching the wind round up the autumn leaves outside. Dina looked the same as she always looked on a Sunday: her angular frame softer in comfort clothes than lawyer clothes, hair fanned out in a ponytail, her face sleepy and kinder without makeup. You couldn't tell what had happened by looking at her. Somehow, Natalie had imagined that you could.

"We should talk about what's going on," Dina said.

"Okay," Natalie said.

"I'm very angry and I'm very hurt. But I'm all right."

"I know." Natalie couldn't think of what else to say.

"Almost half of married couples get divorced. I feel awful, but I'm not special. Do you know what I mean?"

"I think so."

"Some milk would go well with these pretzels, wouldn't it?" Dina went into the kitchen and came back with two glasses. "I'll be a single mother now. I've always thought that would be the hardest thing."

"I'll help you. I'll babysit more, if you want me to."

"Thanks." Dina sighed. "People expect me to fall apart. They expect me to rail about what pigs men are, to break down in public, this pathetic woman, this poor mother, this tough lady lawyer—look at her now. I won't do it. Do you understand?"

"Yes," Natalie said. She wasn't sure that she did, but whatever Dina wanted her to understand, she wanted to understand it too.

Just before Natalie's mom came to pick her up, Dina suggested that next Saturday she and Matt and Natalie could go to New York, maybe stand in the half-price ticket line and get tickets to a show. Natalie hesitated. She hadn't planned to mention William, felt ashamed to, especially now, but she couldn't not tell her aunt.

"I'm supposed to hang out with this guy next Saturday."

"You are?"

"He asked me on Friday. But I can tell him we could do it another time."

"No, no." Dina smiled. "Come here."

Dina's hug was like no one else's. It wasn't the kind of hug where you leaned in, just for a second, and then back out. Dina gripped you so hard you had to remember to breathe, and it made you think about how your body existed alone in space almost all of the time.

"Dating," she said. "I guess I might have to learn to do it again. You'll need to tell me what to do."

Since then, seventeen years ago, Dina had gone on many dates, a few of her relationships lasting for a year or more. Rob got married to a hygienist and had a child with her. But Dina had never married or lived with anyone again. The weekend before the test results came back showing stage 4 stomach cancer, she'd gone on a first date with a man she'd liked instantly. While she was trying to digest the news, he called and left a message asking her out again. She didn't call him back.

"I've never blown someone off like that," she told Natalie during the first round of chemo. "I feel bad about it. But what could I say? *I'm sorry, I'm having cancer right now. Come see me in the hospital.*"

"You could still call him," Natalie said.

What if—as in one of those romantic cancer movies—Dina had a real chance at love now, sick as she was? Maybe this man would cling to her bedside, worship the beautiful spirit beneath the failing body.

"No," Dina said. "No one wants that."

The heartbeat filled the warm room with a whumping sound. Outside it was February, the kind of record-breaking winter that provided a steady source of material for conversations with people in waiting rooms. So cold, so much snow, so many days without sun. The baby would be born in a kinder season.

"A hundred forty beats per minute," the technician said. "That's perfectly fine."

A fetal ultrasound was perhaps the only medical procedure that could be seen as joyful, though of course it could reveal terrible news too. But inside Natalie, things seemed to be going well. The fetus was projected on the screen, its organs and appendages announced and praised.

"You said you want to know the gender, right?" the technician asked.

"Yes," Natalie said. Ian took her hand. He'd told her he didn't have a preference. She was hoping for a girl, not because of the so-called mother/daughter bond, or because she liked girly things, but because as a girl herself she'd imagined having her own girl one day, and it meant something to have that fantasy fulfilled.

The technician zoomed in on an area, rendering it inscrutable to Natalie. After the birth, they would never want to see inside in this way again. The kid should be all smooth skin and ruffled hair, baby-plump flesh and solid limbs. Never the white bones, the pulsing organs. Never the body beneath its protective layer.

"Definitely a girl," the technician said. "See those three dots? Those are the female genitals." Natalie nodded, though she hadn't really seen them.

"We'll get pictures of this?" Ian asked.

"The radiologist will bring them in. She'll look over the results, but I don't anticipate anything out of the ordinary. Congratulations."

The technician handed Natalie a paper towel to wipe the goop off her belly and left to find the radiologist. It was pleasingly cavelike in the room, the light a muted purple, as if a nearby lava lamp were oozing out blobs of wax.

"A girl," Ian said. "Her features looked kind of feminine, don't you think?"

"Sure," Natalie said.

"Dahlia, then?"

"Dahlia."

They hadn't decided on a boy's name. Devin was one idea, Daniel another. The Jewish tradition was to name a child in honor of a relative who had passed away—none of that goyish So-and-So-Junior stuff. A shared first letter would suffice between the namesake and the baby. Natalie wondered what the Orthodox rabbis would say if the relative's death hadn't happened yet. Would they adjust the rule considering the context, sign off on a couple's choice to name a baby after a dying woman, or would they, in their stickler rabbinical way, insist that not taken by God yet was as good as alive?

C raggy and steep on a cliff above the Hudson River, Fort Tryon Park was wilder than Central Park, less cultivated by picnickers and bicyclists. Natalie's mom and Dina had grown up a short walk away from the Heather Garden entrance to Fort Tryon. This park had been Dina's escape when she was feeling angry or depressed. She came for the fortress of trees and the boats inching down the river. She came for the Cloisters, the medieval branch of the Metropolitan Museum of Art, built from the imported remains of French abbeys: a museum packed with so many centuries-old treasures, she'd told Natalie, that she found it impossible to remain stuck in twentieth-century gloom.

She was about to go into hospice care in Connecticut, and Natalie had driven the two of them here first. She unpacked the two lawn chairs from the trunk of Ian's car and set them on the grass near a patch of daffodils. The shiny trees all boasted new leaves. It was the first week of April, stunningly pretty and temperate after the crushing winter. The turning of seasons felt oppressive to her now. If this was to be Dina's last spring, better that it had stayed winter. She opened the car door and helped Dina over to the chair. At seven months pregnant, Natalie knew she shouldn't try to bear the weight of another woman, even one as skinny as Dina was now. At seven months pregnant, she would do what she pleased.

From her lawn chair Dina asked, "How are you feeling? About the birth." The way she spoke now, she seemed to use all of her breath, all of her remaining power, just to form the words.

"I don't know. Weird. I told you we're taking a class? Every time the teacher proposes one of her 'journey to birth' exercises, I can't help groaning. Ian gets annoyed with me. And we have homework. For next week we have to bring in a song that somehow embodies our vision of the birth experience."

"What will you bring?"

"'Billie Jean,' I think. Just to provoke the teacher."

Dina smiled her cracked smile. "I barely remember it. Such pain. But I wasn't there somehow. Not the best day of my life. The birth is just what has to happen."

What had been the best day of Dina's life? Natalie couldn't bring herself to ask that.

"I've got a song," Dina said. "For my journey, not yours."

For a moment Natalie had an impossible thought: Dina

was going on a trip. But no—she was just being ironic. She was DNR. She planned to be cremated.

"Pink Floyd. 'The Great Gig in the Sky.' You know it, right?"

"Yeah, it's beautiful."

"That male voice, so calm, 'I am not frightened of dying, any time will do. Why should I be frightened of dying?' Then that woman wailing. So alive. I always wanted her voice."

"I wanted to tell you." Natalie stopped, sunk her head in her hands, forced herself to keep speaking. "We're going to name her Dahlia. And her Hebrew name will be Devorah—for you."

Natalie lifted her head, opened her eyes. It was all still there: grass, trees, river, people.

"I like that so much," Dina said.

It happened the way Natalie had hoped, if you could hope for such a thing: Dina going quietly, with Matt by her side, a few days before Natalie's due date. She hadn't really wanted to be there when Dina died, and yet, when the call came, she felt that she'd missed something it was unforgivable to miss. Though she couldn't have done anything, couldn't have changed anything.

Then the funeral, the week of sitting shiva at her parents' house. This time she didn't run away, like she had when her grandmother died, but did as the others did, sat in a chair and listened politely.

"She was so smart."

"What perfect June weather."

"She was so independent."

"Did you know we're going to Australia?"

"She was so strong."

"Have some more potato salad."

People hugged Natalie gently and said reasonable things: "Bet you're ready for that baby to pop out already."

"What a shame your aunt didn't get to meet her."

Natalie said "Yes." She said "I know." If this world without Dina seemed a fake, why not be nice, why not be agreeable? Why not let cousin Michael get her a pillow to ease her neck, a footstool to rest her legs? Why not smile when Great-Aunt Ethel said that having a child was the best thing you could do, the best thing she'd ever done?

At forty-one weeks, Natalie went into the hospital for a stress test. If she passed it, her doctor was willing to let her keep going for another week. But the nurse came back with the test results: she'd failed. Her amniotic fluid was too low. Natalie hadn't been able to imagine what the pain of labor would be like. Now she didn't have to.

"Tell me when you can't feel any pressure here," the surgeon said, and a minute later, Natalie couldn't feel anything. Ian sat in a chair by her head, the curtain shielding below her waist. He'd been excited to watch her push out the baby. This he didn't want to see. After a while the surgeon said, "Would you like to meet your daughter?"

Looking at Ian's glowing face beneath the surgical cap, Natalie felt as if it were really to him that this remarkable thing was happening. The doctors pronounced the baby in perfect shape and delivered her to her father. Natalie's arms were shaking too much from the epidural to be of any use. Ian cradled Dahlia, holding her up so that Natalie could see. The baby looked rosy and peaceful, with black tufts of hair and blue-gray slanted eyes. It wasn't then— touching the tiny hands with trembling fingers, or fitting the pursed lips around her nipple, or seeing her mom weep, her dad kiss Dahlia's forehead. It wasn't until late that night—when Natalie lay in the hospital bed, a patient recovering from abdominal surgery—that she knew she'd been wrong.

Ian was asleep on the hard cot by the window. Dahlia was asleep in the metal bassinet. It wasn't Natalie's choice to make, but still she should have chosen, in that terrible game of hypothetical choice, to bring her baby to Dina— for however little time was left—and let them breathe the same air. She had been wrong to elevate a ritual of grief over a moment of joy. She didn't really believe in the Judaism of old, but she believed in women, in girls, watching the candles burn all the way down on the same menorah, generation to generation.

The Dissembler's Guide to Pregnancy

Facts & Figures

He was twenty-nine, seven years younger than me, and
we'd been together for over a year or not at all, depending
on how you calculated it. Finn didn't call me his girlfriend,
or introduce me to his family, or suggest plans beyond next
Saturday night. But he played me folk songs he'd composed
himself on his guitar, baked cakes for friends' birthdays,
teared up at Pixar movies, and washed my feet in the
bathtub. Children adored him—he worked twenty hours a
week at a preschool, for God's sake. Decades of potential
eligibility, of far-in-the-future fatherhood, awaited him,
while, fertility-wise, I was like an aging ballplayer: how
many years could I have left?

My mother sent me articles about how to freeze your
eggs. I had nothing against the idea in theory. Biology, not
to mention patriarchy, levied a fundamental injustice by
giving women a ticking clock and men a remote control
with a pause button, and why shouldn't women do what
they could to subvert that system? But the thing was, I'd

already found the man I wanted to have a baby with, and we were having sex—delicately-dancing-up-to-it-and-talking-long-into-the-night-afterward sex, which I wanted to keep having for the rest of my life.

When I told Finn I was pregnant, I pointed out that the pill is, on average, ninety-one percent effective. "So nine out of a hundred women get pregnant on the pill." I told him that almost half of all pregnancies in the U.S. are unplanned. "Half! Jesus!"

The times I'd seen Finn get upset, he didn't become stonily silent or passive-aggressive or accusatory. He got pensive instead. That's how I could tell—well, one of a million reasons—that he would be a great dad.

"I'm not ready for this," he said. "I'm almost thirty, but I still feel like a kid."

"I know." I squeezed his hand and modulated my voice to an appropriately hesitant register. "But maybe we could make it work?"

Conception

On the Fourth of July, we'd dragged a futon onto the tiny deck of Finn's fifth-floor studio apartment and pressed against each other under a blanket as we gazed up at the fireworks being set off from the park. I'd always wanted to make love while watching fireworks, and it was as I'd imagined, with the exploding lights in the sky like the explosions inside our bodies, bright colors illuminating everything before fading out into kaleidoscopic dust. "I love you," Finn breathed, just after he came. I was stunned; he'd never said that before. We'd been seeing each other off and on for ten months, and Finn had told me—in the gentle, reasonable voice he might use with three-year-olds resistant to naptime—that he understood my wishes and concerns, and there wasn't anyone else, but he didn't want a relationship right now. I was willing to take what I could get.

As the moment calmed, I said, "I love you too," but while his declaration had been a radiant burst vanishing into the night, mine stuck around like a red flare. The sky churned with the cloudy residue of powder and metal, carbon and hydrogen. And then the fireworks were over and we were left with the stars.

I thought of a poem, one of the few poems I had memorized and could summon up whole. "The More Loving One," by W. H. Auden—four quatrains in iambic tetrameter, about stars but not really. I'd been assigned to read it in college, and the meaning eluded my nineteen-year-old brain, until my literature professor explained it in class. The professor was probably younger than I am now, and he had a handsomely brooding air and alternately wry and tender views on literature and life, which he confided as if we students were his intimates. Naturally, I was in love with him.

Humans are captivated by stars, but the feeling is not mutual. And this state of things, the poem tells us, is preferable to the opposite scenario: "How should we like it were stars to burn / With a passion for us we could not return?" We would not like it, Auden says, in so many (so few!) words.

Better to be the lover than the beloved, if one must choose between them. Amid the imbalance of the universe, let me be the one lit up with want.

Nothing really changed after that. We continued seeing each other without discussing the future or even defining the now. I didn't try to pressure him into more; only a crazy lady would make demands of a star. But I staked my greater lovingness as a kind of claim. I aimed my telescope toward the celestial being yet to be born.

Nutritional Supplements

Finn came back from a shift at the preschool fretting about the state of childcare in America. "Parents are paying a ton, and childcare workers barely make enough to live on. But we can't have the government helping people out—no, that would be socialism."

So let's move to Europe, I wanted to say, but restrained myself.

I suspected this was Finn's way of expressing concern about the financial strain of parenthood, and some reassurance was in order. As the development director for a community foundation, I had a stable job with a salary sufficient to meet my needs and those of a child, as long as we lived frugally. I knew how to manage money and how to wheedle it out of other people. What worthier things could they spend it on than public art, and food for the hungry, and afterschool programs for low-income kids?

"Yeah, it's criminal, but I'll be the breadwinner, okay?"

When I told him I was pregnant, though he was too polite to mention it, I'm sure he must have been thinking: there goes my dream. He wanted to become a great singer-songwriter—and I wanted that for him too. Think of those lovely songs Paul Simon wrote for his children.

"You're sure you want to do this?" he asked. He had also been too gentlemanly to directly suggest the possibility of abortion.

"The circumstances are not ideal," I said. "But there might not be another chance. I'm thirty-six. 'Advanced maternal age,' they call it."

He sighed, presumably not in reaction to unflattering medical jargon used for women past their childbearing prime. "You've seen a doctor?"

"Not yet. There's not much to do at this point. Just take prenatal vitamins the size of horse pills. I hate swallowing pills."

He patted my thigh sympathetically.

The birth control pills were such smidges that I hadn't minded taking them for over a decade. Now I had to choke down one of these monsters every day. I did it by imagining a baby as I slugged my glass of water—one of those clear-eyed wonders they use in magazine ads for investment firms and car insurance, looking devastatingly wise in his or her fledgling innocence. It didn't always work, though, and sometimes I'd spit the pill out into my hand, gasping and heaving, conjuring the threat of a malnourished, birth-defect-ridden baby, until I finally forced it down. And sometimes, dutifully swallowing the horse pills, I thought about how I'd neglected those other, tinier ones. Then, I imagined the scores of women who hadn't wanted babies, who'd been forced into motherhood by men—because of their time and place in history, because of religion and social convention and poverty and rape. I worked myself up into a righteous frenzy so populated with brutish men and maltreated women that a slender, mild-mannered twenty-nine-year-old male couldn't be spotted amid the throng.

Growth Chart

Throughout the first trimester and into the second, the misnamed plague called morning sickness (it was not limited to the morning) descended upon me. Throwing up, which had only ever happened to me a handful of times before, each occasion marked by horror and a particular food I was never able to eat again, became an almost daily event. My breasts ached, especially when I went out in the cold. Underneath the down parka, I banded my wool scarf around my chest instead of my neck, and still my nipples stung like frostbitten fingertips. My pelvic region quaked: strange throbbings, sudden pullings, subterranean pangs.

The consolation was a magic bean expanding in placental water, growing slowly toward the light. On the nights Finn

stayed over, he lay beside me with headphones on while I
fell asleep early, as if knocked out by some fairy-tale potion.
At work I bookmarked a website that compared the baby's
weekly dimensions to fruit and other dainty foods.

It was a poppy seed, a peppercorn, a pomegranate seed,
a blueberry.

Sometimes I thought my ballooning body was beautiful.
I climbed up naked on the edge of the bathtub, trying
not to lose my balance as I ogled myself in the medicine
cabinet mirror. I liked the way the skin stretched so tightly
over my belly. I liked how my small breasts had plumped
up. I even liked the curious brown line that had emerged
right down my middle, running from the bottom of my rib
cage to the top of my pelvic bone, as if I were, for some
mysterious purpose, being divided in half. I wanted to have
this baby for all the reasons people want to have babies:
to carry around a warm bundle with a brand-new face; to
witness the dawning of all kinds of consciousness; to laugh
more; to learn things I'd forgotten; to celebrate birthdays
instead of lamenting them; to not miss out on the meaning
of life—that is, to continue it, a purpose that could seem
utterly banal if one was standing, guts emptied, in front of
a toilet bowl.

Cranberry, cherry, kumquat, passion fruit.

Midway through the second trimester, when the nausea
faded, pregnancy-related carpal tunnel began to set in.
The fingers on both hands tingled; my wrists hung heavy
as saddlebags. I had a hard time operating the gearshift
in my car, turning the crank on the can opener, gripping

my toothbrush. The ob-gyn said the condition could last throughout the pregnancy and for a while afterward. "But I try not to speculate too much," she said. "Every pregnancy is different."

"So it might go away?" I asked hopefully.

"Probably not," she said.

On the nights Finn slept at his place, I sat awake in bed, pressing an ice pack to my throbbing wrists. Alone in my apartment, I felt panic sprout up like a time-lapsed tree in spring, popping open bud after bud. What if Finn wanted to be on his own forever? What if he dropped me and became merely a devoted weekend father? Or disappeared completely into another life, another family? I would be a single parent. I thought that I could handle being a single parent, but what had I done to prepare for such a formidable status? I used to babysit in high school. I'd watched a couple of TV shows that featured single parents and cheered them along. I raised money for an organization that helped children, but I didn't actually spend time with them. I was like one of those idiots who run for political office on the platform of not being a politician.

Nectarine, mango, artichoke, papaya.

Quickening

Before the word *pregnant* came to mean *with child,* it meant *full of meaning. Pregnant pause. Pregnant matter.* Rich with implication and significance.

Before the word *quick* meant *fast,* it meant *lively, alive.*
The quick or the dead. To be *quick with child,* to experience
quickening: the first detectable fetal movements.

"What does it feel like?" Finn asked, his hand swirling my
stomach.

"Like a swish. A darting minnow. My little tadpole."

I'd had a standard ultrasound at nineteen weeks, but I
asked the technician not to tell us boy or girl. It seemed
more exciting that way: back to the days of blue and pink
cigar bands, the dramatic reveal announced by the doctor
holding the newborn aloft.

Finn pulled up my shirt and addressed the belly. "You're
gonna start hearing in there soon. Maybe you already can.
Should I sing to you? A little Pete Seeger?" He sang the first
verse of "If I Had a Hammer" in his sweet, rousing voice.
"Can you hear me? Testing. I'm tricking you into thinking
your dad is a famous folk singer."

He sang the rest: hammer of justice, bell of freedom,
song about love between brothers and sisters. I hadn't
heard him do this number before—a favorite from my
childhood, though my parents wouldn't have sung it to me
in the womb or beyond. Not hippie bell-ringing types, my
parents. Their wary approach to the world was the main
thing they had in common, and they'd been married forty
years. Finn and I were so much more compatible (I was just
saying, to no one at all).

As a girl, I used to stick a pillow under my shirt to see
how I'd look pregnant. It was all riches, all romance
in that lexicon, to imagine being grown up and pretty,

with a baby kicking in my belly, and so loved by my husband, and carrying none of my own mother's flaws or disappointments.

Now I was grown up and looked like my mother and didn't have a husband, and what was under my shirt was not pillow-soft but startlingly hard, an armored vehicle enclosing the precarious, shape-shifting being inside. If it were to stop now, the word *stillbirth* would be used. Quickening replaced by a permanent stillness. I didn't see how I could become accidentally pregnant again.

Pregnancy, as I'd come to know it so far, was not quick at all, but ungainly and uncertain and weird and slow.

Baby Registry

Please give this child a strong stomach, an infectious laugh, an independent spirit.

A love of words, numbers, people, and solitude.

A fear of poisons, reckless driving, guns—and nothing else.

Make him or her contemplative but not to the point of fretfulness.

Make him or her generous but not to the point of self-effacement.

Let this child inherit Finn's features, especially his eyes, nose, and mouth.

And his trim, athletic limbs.

His capable hands.

Will-taste-anything tongue.

Un-noteworthy feet.

Ability to not shower for several days and still smell
okay, even good in an earthy way.

His musical talent—yes, especially that.

Even his resistance to being pinned down, because
why settle for anything less than a life full of great
adventure?

Let this child inherit an enduring faith in the power of
secular humanism in a world full of racism, sexism,
terrorism, and greed.

If you must, my teeth and/or earlobes would be fine.

Nesting

Seven months along, I stood in the office/guest room/
fitness center in my apartment that was going to become
the nursery, while Finn tested out paint on the walls. Like
the rest of my apartment, the room had been cream-
colored since I'd moved in. Cream was fine for me, but it
didn't seem good enough for the little one. The little one
would want Peach Fuzz or Hearts of Palm or Waterscape
or Optimistic Yellow.

"What's your pleasure?" Finn asked.

I tried to picture each block of color expanded across the
whole room and none of them seemed worthy.

"Could you do a mural? A flowering tree here, moon and
stars there. Maybe a friendly monkey."

"It would look like a little kid painted it. Worse, actually."

"Well, what do you like?"

By which I meant not only what color paint did he prefer, but what would make him want to move permanently into my cream-colored bedroom down the hall. Or we could paint that something else too: Ancient Marble, Wishful Blue, Breathless, Contented. It would have been financially wise, at the very least, for Finn to move in with me, but he was still hanging on to the tiny apartment he had to shell out savings to pay for.

"The apricot," Finn said. "It has a warm feel. And it's striking without being too much."

He was probably right, but still I picked up the Sherwin-Williams color fan deck I'd borrowed from a coworker whose husband was a contractor and sat down on my exercise bike. I fanned out the deck as far as it could go, a wheel of possibilities available for purchase. "Maybe I missed something," I said.

"You know you're never going to find the perfect color."

"I'm not?"

"The more you stare at that thing, the more you're not going to find it. Just choose something and go with it and it'll be what it is."

I wanted to read everything into that declaration: his change of heart, his marriage vow.

The following weekend I stationed myself at a coffee shop with a book while Finn painted the room. I'd bought zero-VOC latex paint, but he still sent me away. "Go inhale espresso instead. You can buy me dinner later."

In the pages of the book I was reading on education reform in inner cities, I kept seeing him, shirtless, with a paintbrush in his hand, like it was a transcendent vision, a life commitment. As if the choice between Sunrise and Afterglow made all the difference in the world.

Birth Plan

The pregnancy books said childbirth doesn't have to be scary, doesn't have to be clinical, doesn't even have to be painful (it's a matter of redefining pain as at-one-with-the-universe woman strength). They said knowledge is power; and readiness is all; and you should trust your medical professionals; and you shouldn't trust your medical professionals; and why not do Kegel exercises in your office chair; and it's best to avoid caffeine; and there's nothing wrong with a daily cup of coffee to keep you going, girlfriend; and if you find yourself craving charcoal, chalk, dirt, or other nonedible things, try gum, iron pills, or therapy instead; and animals go off on their own to give birth because they know what they need; and your partner may make a great birth coach or he may faint in the delivery room; and you might want to get a doula (from the ancient Greek, meaning *female slave*); and the day your baby is born will be the most momentous day of your life; and there are a number of things that might go wrong, just so you know.

I'd seen my share of birth scenes in movies, and they all seemed fake, even absurd. Jump cut from anguished bellowing woman to shining sweet baby. I didn't buy the tonal shift—horror flick, then sap fest. The new mother suddenly serene and blissful after what she'd just been through. Seeing the new dad cradle his infant, though, all loving and responsible—that's what got me.

We took a tour of the birthing center at the hospital, visiting the waiting room with its massive windows and view of a manmade duck pond, and the hallways decorated with bad art, where I might stroll to move labor along. The tour guide showed off a triage room, a labor and delivery room, and a surgical suite, all sterile chic.

"We just finished our big renovation this past fall. So everything's new and sparkling and our patients tell us it's like staying in a nice hotel."

One thing I liked about writing grants was that you could put your hyperbolic claims in writing rather than having to hear how suspicious they sounded in the air.

"Postpartum, you'll be assigned a private or semi-private room, depending on space. So another mom might be in there with you. There's a fold-out couch if partners want to stay, but they're not to use the bathrooms in the room. Public restrooms are down the hall." The tour guide looked pointedly at Finn.

"Mmhm," he said.

"After delivery, mom and baby are kept safe with security bands both of you will wear. Should anyone attempt to take a baby out of the Birth Center, an alarm sounds and elevators and staircases lock automatically. If the baby needs to go to the nursery, mom and baby's bands are matched to ensure the right baby is delivered back to the right mom."

It had not occurred to me that anyone might try to steal my baby or that I might get the wrong baby. My concerns were of a more basic sort. How was I going to push this watermelon-sized creature out of me? And when it was out, would the three of us call ourselves a family?

"Any questions?" the tour guide asked suddenly.

We couldn't think of any.

On our way back to the parking garage, Finn said, "What if you gave birth out in the woods?"

"Romantic," I said.

"It's like, hey, look at our fancy facilities. You better not mess them up."

"Yeah. But you'll stay over on that couch thing, right?"

"That seems to be my only option."

Finn opened the car door and I maneuvered my unwieldy body into the passenger seat. He got in behind the steering wheel, buckled his seat belt, and began to back out of the spot.

Then I broke down in that embarrassingly female way, where the tears flood out with hiccupping sobs and your nose runs all over the place.

"Hey," Finn said, putting his hand on my leg and then taking it back to negotiate a sharp turn down to the next level. "It's not the Ritz, but I think they know what they're doing here."

"I'm scared," I sniveled.

"Of course."

"I mean I'm trying not to expect anything. I'm not asking you to get down on one knee, but I just can't help wondering. Are we going to be together or not? Are you more than just the baby daddy?"

Finn handed the lot attendant some money and thanked him pleasantly. "Look, we're together right now, aren't we? Let's focus on the most important thing. A healthy baby, right? And we'll take it from there. This whole thing, it wasn't supposed to happen. We're figuring it out as we go."

I pulled crumpled tissues out of the glove compartment and tried to get hold of myself. The plan was, the plan had always been, to stay cool and self-sufficient. There was only one thing I'd needed from him and I'd gotten it; it had flowed into me effortlessly. I wanted other things, yes— I wanted everything—but if you tried to get too much, you might end up with nothing at all.

We were unspooling out of the hospital loop, marked with signs in fire-engine red, past the Women's and Children's Center, the Cancer Center, Adult Emergency. I knew scores of babies were born in the hospital, and that people received lifesaving treatments and came back from the almost dead, but it did not seem to me at the moment that anything good could happen there.

Kick in the Ribs

At thirty-six weeks, inside the belly I carried around like it was an outpost of my body, was an actual baby, nearly fully formed. Aimed head down for sure, because a foot was lodged up under the ribs on my right side, digging into them. I kept pressing my carpal-tunneled hand into the area, trying to nudge the foot out, my first act of gentle but firm (and futile) parenting. The foot would not budge.

Instead of talking or reading or listening to music or having sex, Finn and I fell asleep while watching TV. The baby bump between us, kind of sexy when it was smaller, now just intruded, like a burly cop at a teen party. We watched political pundits argue; and sitcom families insult one another; and twenty-somethings evaluate their romantic partners, call them cutie hotties, and cheating bitches and sons of bitches. A commercial for an antidepressant came on: smiling people doing happy, energetic things, while the warnings running across the bottom of the screen about all the miserable potential side effects made it seem like only an idiot would buy what they were selling. After that commercial ended, we watched one for an anti-aging skin cream: the revolutionary treatment; the woman's face, before and after.

And then, as if awakening to the world's duplicity, Finn asked the question I'd almost convinced myself by now that he would never ask. "You *were* taking the pill, right?"

I kept staring at the TV as if it might suck me in.

Nine months of allowing myself to believe that a cosmic accident—being the more loving one—was some kind of justification for taking matters into my own hands. That the widespread prevalence of gender inequality excused it. That deceit had simply become fate, or restitution. The statistic I'd given, that nine out of a hundred women get pregnant on the pill, required some qualification. In truth, if taken correctly, the pill is ninety-nine percent effective.

The ninety-one percent figure is for "typical use"—meaning women who skip pills, who get wrapped up in their daily lives and make a little mistake sometimes. Hardworking women, who rush out the door in the morning forgetting that itty-bitty necessity; exhausted women, who fall asleep with the lights on; romantically preoccupied women, who drink too many gin fizzes and stay over at their boyfriends' houses, or leave their purses on the bus, or leave town while that flimsy packet of punch-out pills stays behind in the medicine cabinet. Dissembling women, who decide to stop taking the pill without a word to their lovers.

I couldn't look at Finn, his starry eyes, his pensive lips. "Well," I said.

In the nearly two years I'd known him, I'd never seen him get really angry. I guess, up until then, he hadn't had anything to get angry about.

I went to work and worked hard, stayed late, trying to wrap up loose ends before my maternity leave would begin. At home in the apricot nursery, I folded and refolded newborn clothes. I made sure my phone was always fully charged, in case it was time, in case there was anything from Finn. The night the truth came out, when he was sitting next to me in bed, the TV still spewing lies in its cheerful way, I'd said I was sorry a dozen times. I texted it now, cell to cell: *I'm so sorry Finn. Just wanted you to know that again.* He texted back: *Still can't talk to you right now. Lmk when it's time to go to the hospital.*

But what I was most sorry about was that I hadn't said, "Yes, of course I was taking it," and then recited the spiel about the nine out of a hundred women on the pill, the nearly half of all pregnancies in America that were unplanned. I was sorry that although he'd said he loved me, he hadn't *fallen* in love with me, and that he was young enough and eligible enough that the distinction mattered. I was sorry I'd wanted a baby because I was thirty-six, and babies were cute, and pregnant women had seemed like magical beings, and I was afraid of being old and lonely and having no one who belonged to me. Sorry that, for all the inadequacies I saw in myself, I'd always thought I was an honest person, and I was no longer able to think of myself that way. And sorry that, right now, the final countdown to birth felt like the countdown to a rocket ship launch, and rockets could explode in the sky.

Thirty-seven weeks, thirty-eight, thirty-nine. The heartburn was so bad I didn't want to eat much, but I forced something down for dinner every night and then lay in bed with stiff hands, swollen legs, fuzzy brain. As soon as my body assumed a state of semi-relaxation, the baby shuttled into motion, as if we were coworkers operating in tight shifts. One foot jabbed me in the side, and the other continued to dig into my ribs, like it had no intention of leaving. Or like I'd already taught this kid that to get what you want in life, you'd better come out kicking, no matter who you hurt.

Ten Warning Signs of Postpartum Depression

1. Lack of Interest in Your Baby

The baby is a minute old, an hour old, a day, a week. His skin is blotchy and yellowish, his eyes a blurry blue. He's like a woodpecker, bonking his head against your chest, drilling into your breasts, while you have to make like a tree and take it. He's a pirate, with his guttural yawp, his fie-on-this expression, his wholesale seizure of your sleep. Like a disappointed old woman: pinched and furrowed, primed for complaint.

When he's fifteen days old, you change out of one pair of yoga pants and into another, grab the diaper bag, and strap the baby into the car seat. Your mother has flown home to her board meetings, her step classes, and her book club. Your husband is at the office, his shirt unwrinkled, his tie pulled tight. "Be sure to leave the house today," he told you, and so you are leaving, but there's a long list of people and places you can't face. Not your friends who are mothers. Not your friends who aren't mothers. Not the grocery store, the library, the neighborhood.

And so you drive to a dismal apartment building where Alex, just out of college, fourteen years younger than you, has promised banana bread. He had offered to bring it over on his bike, but you told him you needed to get out of the house, and so he invited you here.

Alex opens the door with a smile for the baby, asleep in the car seat. *"Cómo estás?"* he exclaims. "Or, I should say, *Cómo están ustedes?"*

You know each other from Tertulia, a Spanish conversation group that meets Thursday nights at a Mexican restaurant, a group composed mostly of earnest Americans trying to work on their Spanish. Alex, skinny and sweet-faced with a gringo accent, seemed to look up to you simply because, in the hierarchy of nonnative Spanish speakers sitting around the table munching chips and salsa, you were near the top. As a graduate student in comparative literature studying Latin American modernism, you've spent years learning Spanish. You're in the midst of a dissertation on Chilean revolutionary women poets— in the way one can be in the midst of a dissertation for going on five years now. But that is another depression that has, as of fifteen days ago, been upended by the arrival of this other project that won't stand to wait around until you're in the mood to pay attention to it.

"We're all right. How are you?" You're not here to speak Spanish. You're here because you thought you could keep from crying in front of this young, male not-quite-friend.

"Kind of bad, actually," Alex says, as you set the car seat down. "My cat's been missing since last Friday."

"Oh no. What happened?"

"She managed to get out when I was carrying laundry down to the basement and somehow escaped from the building. I put up signs and rode my bike all over, looking for her."

"I'm so sorry."

"She always wanted to be free," he says gloomily. "But wow. You have a baby. How did it go? I mean his—being born?"

You had the childbirth experience you'd wanted, a natural birth: meaning it hurt so much you thought something must be terribly wrong, even though you knew childbirth was supposed to feel worse than anything you'd ever experienced in your life. "I can't do it!" you kept screaming, and the midwife contradicted you gently, and she was right, but when the baby finally came out, you didn't feel triumphant so much as beaten into submission.

"It was okay, I guess. I mean it was good in that he's healthy. I'm sorry. I don't know how to talk about it."

"I understand. I mean I don't understand, of course, so. Do you want to sit down and have some tea?" He gestures toward the single chair at a tiny table and gets the teakettle going in the galley kitchen. The apartment is shabby and dreary, with a stained beige carpet, and nothing on the walls but peeling paint.

"How long have you lived here?"

"Four months. Since I graduated. I could have gotten a nicer place if I lived with roommates, but it's better for me to be alone. Or, I don't know if it's better, but it's what

I can deal with. And they allow cats here. Not that it matters now."

He serves you a large, gooey slice of homemade chocolate chip banana bread. You eat that slice and then another. It's the only food that's tasted good since the birth. Alex perches on a corner of the bed with his tea mug. He tells you that he feels stuck; he's cashing in savings bonds from his dead grandmother and supposedly applying to grad school. He majored in history, but the idea of teaching high school history makes him very afraid. He thinks he should probably try to get a job in a coffee shop, or a bakery, but he's worried that then he'll keep working in a coffee shop or bakery forever. Should he go to grad school? What should he do? And he is sorry to be laying all of this on you.

You tell him that grad school has been bad for you, but it's probably not grad school's fault. You tell him he should find a way to leave the country immediately: go to Latin America, go anywhere exciting and cheap. You tell him you have no wisdom to offer—that age and experience mean only that you are older and have found ways to let years of your life go by.

Too soon, always too soon, the baby wakes and starts gnawing on his fist. In a minute he will realize that his fist can give him nothing. And you're not going to breastfeed him here, in front of Alex.

"I'd better go before he freaks out."

Alex jumps up to open the door, knocking over a stack

of *Mother Jones* magazines balanced on a milk crate. "I can't believe I just talked about my lame stuff when you, you're the one with the amazing new thing—new person."

"No, I, I'm interested." You step into the hallway, gripping the car seat. "That banana bread was delicious. I hope you find your cat."

"Yeah. Well, as you can see, I've got nothing going on. Come by anytime." He touches the baby's clenched hand. "You too."

2. Lack of Energy and Motivation

THINGS TO DO:

· Reflect on the miracle of birth.
· Begin filling out pages in the fancy journal on your nightstand, entitled *Baby's First Year*, recording weight, length, hair color, first impressions, etc.
· Use the stationery printed with Edwardian baby dolls, which you received as a gift, to write thank-you notes for the stationery, the journal, and other adorable gifts.
· Consume oatmeal, oatmeal cookies (special recipe for lactating women), salmon, carrots, fennel seeds, fenugreek seeds, cumin seeds, and garlic in order to (possibly) increase your breast milk supply.
· Keep a round-the-clock chart of the baby's feeding times, sleeping times, and diaper changes, which may help to facilitate the illusion of control.
· Sign up for a postpartum yoga class, or get a

postpartum yoga DVD from the library and follow along, which may help to ease the reality of panic.
· Speak to the baby in Spanish: step one of his bilingual education.
· Read the stack of parenting books on your nightstand.
· Sleep when your baby is sleeping.

THINGS YOU HAVE DONE:
· Lamented the demise of the wet nurse.
· Watched the instructional video for the Moby Wrap Newborn Hug Hold, over and over, and failed to re-create the Moby Wrap Newborn Hug Hold on your own person.
· Read a pamphlet you received in the hospital, entitled *Ten Warning Signs of Postpartum Depression.*
· Cried when your baby was crying.

3. Negative Feelings Toward Your Baby

On the second visit to Alex's apartment, you decide to ditch your modesty and breastfeed, while Alex works in the kitchen, his back discreetly turned. You set the writhing baby on the comforter, unlatch your nursing bra, stick a pillow on your lap, pick up the baby, and attempt to position him once, twice, three times. He grips your nipple with puckered lips. It kills.

You pull him off and try again to aim him just so, to get him to open his mouth wider so it pinches you less. "Big mouth," you whisper hopelessly (the baby understands neither English nor Spanish). "Big mouth."

One more frustrated try—then you give up and let him pinch.

If you're to breastfeed for at least a year, as everyone says you should, that's roughly six times a day for at least 340 more days: a minimum of, say, 2,000 breastfeeding episodes.

These precious early months with your infant: you wish them all away. Let him be sitting in a high chair on his first birthday with a plastic plate of cake, having learned to hold his head up, sit, wield a spoon, and eat unnutritious food— all in the blink of an eye. Let him be drinking from a sippy cup full of milk produced by a cow. Let him be, then, one year closer to the end of his childhood.

Endless suggestions, endless pep talks are available online. It's possible to spend most of the time you're not breastfeeding attempting to fix, or optimize, the endlessly celebrated mammalian superpower. Everyone refers to the latch—*master the latch and all will be well,* as if it's a matter of calling in a good locksmith—but the pain comes not only during a feeding, but afterward, and not only in your nipples, but deep within your breasts and around them, burning into your armpits. You want to press something tightly to your chest at all times, a shield against the throb, and also you want nothing—certainly not a baby—touching you there. The doctors and the lactation consultants respond with mild surprise at your struggle to describe the feeling, not unlike the IT guys manning some help desk you've rushed to in the past, pleading for a resolution, or at least an explanation, to some weird computer problem.

How odd. How strange of the equipment not to operate according to design. A manufacturing fluke, perhaps. Or user error. Either way we can't repair it. So maybe it's your fault. Maybe it's all in your head, not your boobs.

When you're finally done—one down, only 1,999 more to go—Alex offers a cup of chai and some corn muffins. You try to smile as he sets a mug and plate in front of you.

"Do you want me to hold him while you eat?"

Yes. That's what you want.

Cradling the baby awkwardly against his flat, useless, masculine chest, Alex says tenderly, "He looks so content."

And he does, now that he's satiated for the moment, until he's desperate for milk again. And you can't think of a time—no, not in your whole life—when you have ever given another person what he needs so basically and absolutely, while you're left despising your very ability to give.

"Are you okay?" Alex asks, because you're crying into the chai.

"I hate it. I hate breastfeeding." Head in your hands, you can feel him hovering, trying to figure out what to do.

"Well, couldn't you—you could give him formula, right?"

He is twenty-two years old, a childless male. What does he know of it all? *Breast is best. Liquid gold.* Dr. Sears, La Leche League. Maternal guilt, mommy wars. Your husband's urging you to "stick with it; it's so good for the baby." The people online who say if you don't want to breastfeed, you should never have had a child. The medical evidence indicating that breastfed babies experience lower rates of gastrointestinal infections, ear infections, respiratory diseases, asthma, SIDS—and perhaps higher IQs, better achievement in school. The swirly painting in the pediatrician's office of a woman with infants on both breasts—a glorification of the beauty and power of motherhood that makes you want to find a new pediatrician: a bad one, a compromised one, who lets Similac and Enfamil and the rest strew her office with free samples, and will counsel you under the influence of their empires of fake milk.

You nod toward Alex without meeting his eyes. Acknowledged. New topic, please.

4. Worrying About Hurting Your Baby

Before the baby was born, you used to worry that you might drop a baby. Plates, coffee mugs, water pitchers slipped out of your hands sometimes. Babies, too, are breakable.

Now you understand that parents don't drop their babies. Parents are skilled that way. They jiggle and juggle, toss infants back and forth to each other, balance them along with everything else that needs carrying. They don't drop them.

The problem is that you have visions. A bracelet of hands around his throat, a pair of fingertips pinching his nostrils shut. Kitchen knife, pruning saw, refrigerator, oven. Bathtub, washing machine, the trunk of the car. Baby shoved down the laundry chute.

His body is small and compact; it could fit anywhere.

Baby head severed from baby chest. Baby slit open like a sick science experiment.

It's not something you want to do. It's something that occurs to you as within the realm of the horrifically possible.

A life can be started. A life can be ended. The baby knows so little, not even that he has a life. Put a knife to his throat, and he won't be afraid.

You would never do it. You would never do it. You would never do it.

And yet, when you're alone with the baby—husband at work, husband asleep—your heart beats fast, adrenaline gearing up for an unspeakable act.

You pull him in close and tighten your grip. Over and over again, you save him from yourself.

5. Sleeping More or Less than Usual

You come to consciousness in Alex's bed, the baby beside you, eyelids fluttering, sleeping in his arms-up-don't-shoot position. Alex is at his desk in the corner, the back of his neck naked after a close-cropped haircut. You deliberately didn't tell him you noticed, that it looks good. He served treats as usual, and then you apologized for being so tired you could barely keep your eyes open. He offered the bed and you took it.

Close your eyes again, and the world disappears. Isn't that how infants perceive reality? If you can't see it, then it doesn't exist?

Here, in this drab rented apartment, your life doesn't exist. And what about your husband, who has done nothing wrong, or almost nothing? His growing impatience with you, as the gloomy, weeping mother of his child, is understandable. Already you can see that he will be the reasonable grown-up parent, the demonstratively affectionate parent, and you will be something other than that. And that parenthood leaves no time for meaningful conversation between the two parents. Or maybe that's just an excuse for not wanting to discuss how miserable you feel.

Alex swivels around in his chair. "Did you get a good nap?" And you think he is beautiful, both because he's so young and because he won't be for much longer.

"Yeah, thanks. It's a cozy bed."

"I've been sleeping a lot lately." He looks embarrassed. "I guess I'm depressed."

"About the cat?"

"Mmhm. And, you know, not having a job. Or even knowing what I want to do. Being kind of isolated. It's good to talk to you, though."

All your life people have told you that you're a good listener, and you used to feel flattered, but now it seems a dumb thing to be proud of. What if a good listener is just someone who doesn't have anything to say?

"Why?" you press him.

"Why?" There is perhaps nothing more endearing in a man than embarrassment. "I feel like we get each other right now. Maybe that's presumptuous. I wish there was more I could do for you."

You turn your palms up in that what-is-there-to-do way. "Take a nap with us."

You want that, yes, and now you said it. A quick half smile, and his head is on the other pillow, arms pasted to his sides, serious again.

Ridiculous to think of any seductive intent. Your breasts bruised and full of milk. Your vagina a gaping, wounded hole. The baby, prone between the two of you, about to wake up starving any minute now. Plus, you're old.

Close your eyes again; make the world disappear.

And if you turned toward him, then what? He's full of angst and need and tenderness, ready to heap on the person right beside him, simply because you're there.

Down below the baby's curled bare feet, the edge of his hand touches the edge of your hand—touches and doesn't touch it, like a breeze skimming skin.

Then you both pretend to sleep.

6. *Changes in Appetite or Weight*

Pre-pregnancy appetite: Hungry for yummy and
    reasonably nutritious food.
Pregnancy appetite, 1st trimester: Hungry for miso
    soup and orange sherbet.

Pregnancy appetite, 2nd trimester: Hungry for grilled asparagus and French fries.

Pregnancy appetite, 3rd trimester: Hungry for watermelon-lime-cucumber smoothies.

Postpartum appetite: Why the need to eat, to make food for oneself and others, day after endless day?

Pre-pregnancy weight: 130 pounds.

Pregnancy weight: 165 pounds at final prenatal visit.

Postpartum weight: Who gives a shit?

7. Loss of Pleasure

They've always seemed so complicated, affairs. The cheating. The lying: by word and by omission. The requisite self-deception. Of course some people get a thrill from all that. It's never sounded thrilling to you, only another bureaucratic responsibility to manage, like paperwork deliberately misfiled by a sadistic secretary.

The first few times you visited Alex's apartment, you mentioned it to your husband when he got home from work—*he's from Tertulia (you know, Spanish group); recent college grad, not sure what to do with his life; seeking advice (from me, ha); likes babies; likes to bake.* Now your husband no longer asks what you've done all day because he suspects the answer will be tedious, and that you'll recount the tedium in a grim voice; and so there's no need anymore to mention where these tedious, grim activities took place, while your husband eats dinner, and bounces the baby, and reads the newspaper, sometimes all at once.

Other than the cursory bits you told Alex when you first sat next to him at the table of semi-Spanish-speakers in the Mexican restaurant, you've never said anything about your husband. And Alex is also mum on the subject of romantic interests past or present. So it's possible to pretend that two people lying in bed holding each other, while fully clothed and generally unhappy, are simply engaged in some form of primal healing. Skin to skin. Or cotton/poly to viscose/spandex, as the case may be. Various things are discussed. Books. Trips taken and not yet taken. Therapy as mild amusement/narcissistic exercise/waste of money. The unpleasant side effects of antidepressants. The pros and cons of getting a new cat. One afternoon you share suicide stories: you each had a friend, now dead by their own design. Your friend Lydia, a year or so after college, done in by some cocktail of codeine and sleeping pills. Alex's friend Nick, who hanged himself in their junior year of high school. For a little while, the two of them are there in bed with you, the only way they can come alive again, ghosts summoned from fumbling words.

"Hey, is that a smile?" Alex wonders on another afternoon, when the baby's mouth jerks in an upward direction, apropos of nothing, and then jerks back down.

"It's just a puppet smile. A reflex."

"When are they supposed to start smiling for real?"

"Around two months. Pretty soon."

"That'll be so cool."

His own smile makes you think of childhood seen from an honest distance, both lovely and lonely. Birthday cakes, park swings, a secret attic hideaway. And what is the age at which one develops a longing for impossible things?

8. *Lack of Concern for Yourself*

Why not seek out the company of other women, other new mothers: your kind, your kin? Your husband encourages this; so does your mother, and your best friend, who lives on the other side of the country, and whose own child has reached an age—between babyhood and self-entertainment—that no longer allows your friend to talk on the phone, because if the daughter is around, she's always saying "Mommy, Mommy" in the background, and if the daughter isn't around, your friend needs to work and vacuum and sleep, and all the other things she can't do when the daughter is around.

Also, at your eight-week postpartum checkup, the midwife asks how things are going, and you're not able to lie to her well enough, because she has seen you with all your clothes off, screaming obscenities and giving birth to a baby, so you say in a tiny voice, "It's been hard," and she says, "You know, support is out there," and you hate the word *support* because it makes you think of bras and panty hose and girdles: the body parts of women spilling out if not appropriately propped up and contained, and of a sea of concerned faces asking what's wrong and nodding slowly at your answer and thanking you for sharing. But you tell the midwife you'll at least try to go to the new mothers' group that meets on Wednesday mornings in the basement of a Presbyterian church.

When you walk in, seven or eight women are sitting on the worn-out couches, or standing up, jiggling their babies in that habitual mother sway. You'd imagined that it would be like an AA meeting or something: that everyone would state their names, and their issues, and there'd be an air of commiseration and revival in the room. But it's placid here, with a slight aroma of baby shit. One or two of the women smile at you; one or two babies give you the staredown. No one asks your name. You find a corner of a couch next to one of those breastfeeders who doesn't even need to use her hands at all; she's free to gesture as she talks to the woman on her other side, who is busy wrapping her baby into a swaddle.

"He loves the swing," the hands-free breastfeeder says. "I just put him in there and play the nature sounds, and I actually have time to make spaghetti."

"Which one do you have?"

"The Fisher-Price My Little Snugapuppy Cradle 'n Swing. It's expensive but so worth it."

"Wait, say that again." The woman whose expertly swaddled baby now lies like a cozy mummy in her lap pulls out her phone.

"I feel guilty for sticking him in there all the time, though."

"You have to take some time for yourself," one of the standing-up mothers says, and the sitting-down mothers agree.

"As soon as my husband comes home, I get in the tub, and I stay in there for, like, forty-five minutes."

"Mmm, light a candle, and pull out the leftover Halloween candy, and you are set."

And you can see it in the eyes of these women, gently joking and laughing. They aren't stunned by motherhood befalling them like a chronic condition. They don't view breastfeeding as a prison-with-torture sentence. They're not stuck in a codependent relationship with a depressed young man who isn't the father of their child.

Or maybe they are—maybe everyone is—while managing to put on a falsely cheerful face, the way you do, when the mother beside you asks, "Where did you get your baby's cute socks?"

9. Feelings of Worthlessness and Guilt

Think of all the awful stories. The nightmare pregnancies, when the doctors suspect something is wrong, or know something is wrong, but can do nothing to stop it. The baby coming months and months too early: weighing one or two pounds, unable to breathe on his own, bowels obstructed, organs failing. An unexpected event during labor and delivery: asphyxia, hemorrhage, traumatic brain injury. Infants trapped behind glass in the NICU, hooked up to tubes, eyes squeezed shut. Birth defects, surgeries, fatal meningitis.

And the women who can't conceive, who try for years, who spend tens of thousands of dollars on IVF, their hormones jacked up, their hopes jacked up—and still, nothing. The women who carry all the way through—nine months of budding life—and then birth their babies blue and cold, bury them.

These people should have babies right now, should be enjoying them as lovingly as they've imagined in their dreams; while you, with your perfect, "easy" baby, feel trapped inside some vessel that just barely contains your body: an MRI machine; an airport scanner; the replica of a spaceship in a museum, grounded forever.

Also, studies have shown this: Infants of mothers who are clinically depressed are more likely to go on to suffer from depression themselves.

10. Recurrent Thoughts of Death or Suicide

You've come to Alex's apartment with a mission this time. Come through the freezing rain, the beginning of winter, the baby dressed in his nubby brown bear suit with the ears. This morning you picked up the newspaper for the first time since before he was born, the old-fashioned, print newspaper. Your husband doesn't miss a day. When the three of you came home from the hospital, he collected the accumulated newspapers and read them all that night, saving the one from the day of the birth. "He might want to look at it someday," said the new father, sentimental. Today, while the baby watched with half-closed eyes in his bouncy seat, like you were some kind of dreary show, you read. Syria. Afghanistan. International terrorism. U.S. gun violence. Alzheimer's. PTSD. The world still out there, still going down in flames and hanging on. And it felt like the very least you could do—something that would matter to four people or less—to decide, this has to stop.

But first have some poppyseed cake. Alex tells you he has news: an interview scheduled at a coffee shop, the one you can't go to anymore because you've spent too many dismal hours there trying to work on the dissertation. "That's great," you say, with a jealous pang you must tamp down immediately. This could begin a new chapter for him: a job, fun friends, maybe even a girlfriend to eat his cake with.

Then he says, "I dreamt about Nick last night."

"What happened?"

"He was swinging on a trapeze and just talking to me down below, like nothing had happened. But I knew he was dead, and I couldn't figure out how to tell him. For some reason I felt like it was my job to tell him."

The baby starts fussing, and you take him out of his car seat and prop him up on your lap, where he looks intently at Alex. More and more, he has the look of someone who sees what's going on, who's keeping quiet only because he believes that's the wise thing to do.

"I think about death a lot," Alex says. "Nick choosing to be dead. Forever. We'll all be dead forever. It should make us just want to live right now, run outside and feel that, that rain there, like some amazing thing, but somehow it doesn't."

You think about it all the time, too. And now, on top of the dread that rises at the thought of your own end—the real dread of never existing again, not the leaden moments when death seems like some trick to ease pain—there's the unthinkable, too. Babies die. Children die.

It's a kind of grim seduction, Alex your partner in doom, but you can't let it sway you from your decision.

"So, I have to say something." A pause, but not too long. "I feel like I shouldn't come over anymore." He looks away, stirring the spoon in his mug of hot chocolate, and you have to push past it now: chug-a-chug-chug.

"I care about you. I really do. This has been a bad time for me, and you've—I've looked forward to seeing you."

Ignore the pang of his bent head.

"But look. If you were married to me, would you want me to be going over to some other guy's place and lying in his bed, being miserable, with him?"

Throw a dog a bone: "We can still see each other at Tertulia."

"You never go anymore," he says.

"I will. I'll—once everything settles down a little."

Though probably you won't, probably things won't settle down. Some people say it's better when the child gets older, and others say it's just different.

You could tell him, "You have your whole life ahead of you." Or, "I'm not doing you any good." Or, "Some woman soon is going to notice how great you are." But of course those things are patronizing, and they would also require more openhearted generosity than you feel right now. If only the damn cat were still around, and you could pull her away from her feeding dish, or drag her out from under the bed, and place her in Alex's arms—a soft, warm body to love—but she's been gone for ten weeks now. She has some new life, or else she's dead.

You stand up with the baby tucked under your arm and grab the car seat without bothering to strap him into it. Go quickly now, go, while Alex sits on his bed with his head down like a chastened child, like Rodin's *The Thinker* in jeans and a flannel shirt. With your free knuckle, you bump him on the shoulder.

"Take care, okay? Good luck with the interview. Thanks for everything."

You manage to get the door open and shut it behind you, start lumbering down the dingy stairwell, like a callous brute, a petty thief. You think of the way Alex would stroke the baby's hands so gently, exclaiming over the tiny opals of his fingernails. And then a vision comes: the baby all grown up into a young man, about Alex's age, a sensitive young man, a young man in love for the first time, and holding within himself the silent wonder of that.

On the second-floor landing you stop to rest for a moment, and another vision comes, one of the terrible ones: hurtling the baby down the stairs, his head cracking on the cement floor. The screams, the blood, the broken body. You squeeze him into your aching chest, breathing hard against the panic—and your son, in your arms, gazes up at the light fixture suspended from the ceiling, the way he's looked at light for as long as you've known him: like it's a marvel, a celestial sign, the first miracle of creation.

Welcome to Your Family

Christmas music at the mall, plastic reindeer in the neighborhood. Cards crowd the mantel with pictures of everyone's merry children, sending tidings of joy and minor sports triumphs. At the airport, the holiday travelers funnel through—the excited, the weary, the primed-for-disappointment. Alice, the baby, travels from room to room in a portable bassinet, a six-week-old whirl of light and movement, her parents' faces looming large and important, like in an Ingmar Bergman film. Someone has sent her a red-and-green knit hat with a bell. Someone else has sent her a board book called *Baby's First Hanukkah*.

Four years ago, Jack Keeling left his wife and his software development job and began teaching math at a progressive private high school. Tracy Goldman, who taught English there, offered her advice and support. They went out for beers on Friday afternoons, and then began spending the weekends grading together, shoving stacks of student essays and trig tests aside to have sex on Tracy's couch. Two summers later they married at the courthouse, with the assistant principal and her husband serving as witnesses. Jack didn't want to suffer through a second wedding. Tracy had never wanted one to begin with.

So now, over this winter break spanning Christmas and New Year's, their families are coming together to meet the baby, and also to meet one another for the first time. There's Jack's brother Barrett, his wife Michelle, and kids Christina and Luke. A blond, big-boned, toothy clan: the adults outfitted with it's-all-good smiles, the kids on the verge of adolescent blowout. They squeeze into Jack and Tracy's bungalow: the pull-out futon in the upstairs office for Barrett and Michelle, sleeping bags on the floor of the basement family room for Christina and Luke.

Tracy's family is stashed a few doors down, at the house of some neighbors away for the holidays. There's Tracy's mother Ruth, who carries her widowhood like a hernia. Tracy's sister Jessica, husband David, and six-year-old son Ari. A slight, brooding, olive-skinned trio, as dedicated to sulking as the Keelings are to aggressive cheer.

And finally, staying at a hotel—a nice one, with fluffy robes and chocolates on the pillows—Jack's parents, Francine and Nicholas. They are pasty-skinned, in Brooks Brothers clothes. They have money they don't mind spending on their own comfort.

"It's supposed to be a vacation," Jack had said before the Christmas plans were set, when they were counting their daughter's life in days. "Do we really want to have everyone at once?"

"Who do you want to say no to?"

"How about all of them. Just to be fair."

Tracy has her reservations, too. She's met Jack's parents three times now, and they are the sort of couple whose tense relationship with each other inevitably chills the room. Her own parents' bickering was warmer, sillier, often ending with her father pinching her mother's cheeks into a smile. Now that he's gone, there's no leavening influence on her mother's gloomy nature.

"Don't worry, she's our decoy." Tracy stroked the baby's cone head. "We'll hand her over and go hole up in the bedroom. Let everyone get to know one another, or kill one another, or whatever."

"Did you hear that, Alice?" Jack cupped his hands into a megaphone. "We're sending you out as our envoy. Just call if you need a wire transfer. Or military assistance."

Alice started in with her frantic headbanger moves, which meant it was time for Tracy to unlatch the giant nursing bra. She braced herself for the pain the lactation consultant told her she shouldn't have if the baby was feeding correctly. Jack sat back against the couch pillows and watched Tracy wince.

"Remember, she's the boss," the ob-gyn had said to him at one of Tracy's final prenatal visits when they were discussing the birth plan. How was he supposed to respond to that? *Yes, ma'am. If she changes her mind and demands an epidural, I'll bring it in on a tray with a cup of coffee and a vase of fresh flowers.* A month later he sat uselessly in the hospital room for hours, patting Tracy's back while she sucked wild-eyed on popsicles and screamed her labor screams. He'd wanted to seize power, demand a stop to this barbaric ordeal. What was wrong with a nice, efficient C-section? He couldn't help feeling that his wife, the CEO, was dying, and he was just an incompetent, low-level employee, watching it happen.

They overwhelm the small living room—the Keelings and the Goldmans—three generations of eyes and mouths, hair and noses, skin tone and face shape. The baby has been scrutinized for inherited traits and deemed a mongrel by Nicholas, her paternal grandfather. In her Christmassy hat, she perches on Tracy's mother's lap, an air of aloofness in her rainwater eyes. Ruth removes the hat, smooths Alice's blond fuzz. It upsets her, the tree in the corner, delicately adorned and unassuming though it is (tiny white lights, a laughing Buddha instead of an angel on top). She still can't accept that such a thing stands in her daughter's house. The fact that Jack never went to church growing up and sees Jesus as nothing more than a do-gooder type who came to an unfortunate end makes it only a little bit better for Ruth.

"You're Jewish," she'll whisper later to the baby, when they can be alone. "Aleeza. Which means joyful." Aleeza would be Alice's Hebrew name. But Ruth knew there'd been no naming ceremony, no rabbi's blessing. The child was adrift in this world.

"My turn," Barrett says, sticking his arms out. "Hand her over." And Ruth reluctantly relinquishes her granddaughter.

"What do you think, hon?" Barrett addresses Michelle. "Should we make another one?"

Michelle smiles with her preternaturally white teeth. "I always wanted three."

"Oh my God," Christina says.

"Aren't you too old?" Luke says, which makes Barrett laugh and Michelle's smile waver.

Christina and Luke, thirteen and eleven, are used to spending winter break at their other grandparents' house, in Florida, at the beach. This year they're stuck in a small Ohio town instead, in a house that doesn't even have a TV. They have three cousins already, on their mother's side, close to them in age, and with the benefits of a Ping-Pong table, the latest generation Xbox, a cupboard full of nonorganic snack food, and parents too preoccupied with their own affairs to worry about what the kids are doing.

The little boy, Ari, technically not their cousin, hangs shyly around Luke, hoping for attention from this boy almost twice his age and height, who carries around his own phone and has a dog back at home. Ari would like to have a brother, an older brother, if such a thing were possible, through some form of time travel perhaps. He isn't exactly sure how babies are made, but he knows it has something to do with the mother and father being close to each other, loving each other. His own don't sleep in the same bed anymore. Before the cleaning lady comes over, his mom takes the sheets off the couch in the family room so it won't look like his dad has been sleeping there.

"So what does everybody want for Christmas?" Nicholas asks in his booming Santa-Claus-for-hire voice.

"Not everybody's Christian," Christina says.

"He meant Christmas in the secular, materialistic sense," Jack says. "Right, Dad?"

"Everyone's so sensitive these days." Nicholas looks at Luke, as if his grandson will back him up on this assessment. "No one's opposed to presents, right? Everyone's getting presents?"

"They'd better be," Luke says. "And not cheap educational crap either."

"Good health," Ruth mumbles, from her corner of the couch. "That's all we should wish for." It's been nearly two years since her husband died from the cancer that invaded his brain. If he were here, he would lie next to her in bed later that night, eloquently bemoaning the shallowness of these people. *Oh, Ruthie,* he would sigh. *When the Israelites came out from Egypt, they had nothing at all.*

By ten o'clock on Christmas morning, the living room is a wreck—wrapping paper, ribbons, cards, gift tags— all tossed aside in the rush to get to the goods, which pile up in colorful, half-forgotten heaps. Midway through the rampage, Alice starts crying, which gives Tracy an excuse to leave the room and go nurse her: a questionable privilege. Though she's finally toughened up a bit to the job required (now she understands the origin of the expression *tough titties*), it still feels more unpleasant than plucking her eyebrows. What is this breastfeeding bliss she's heard tell about?

Five minutes in, her sister knocks on the bedroom door. Jessica is skinny as ever in her eighties-style denim jacket and jeans, a look that used to be cool but that now screams suburban Jewish mom who's trying too hard. They haven't talked, just the two of them, since Jessica arrived. And it's been years since they've been close. They used to sit on each other's beds while Jessica, three years older, would warn about all of the boys Tracy should steer clear of in a way that made Tracy ache to feel their depraved hands on her skin. Jessica was bold and forthcoming then—not so nice to Tracy as a general rule, but her freely dispensed worldly wisdom made up for it. Tracy was the one who loved to read, but it was Jessica who could tell stories. And then she left home, went to college and business school, got married, and became tight-lipped and conventional.

"She seems to be nursing well," Jessica says, leaning over Tracy and Alice in the glider. "So sweet. I miss it."

"Really? I can't wait to go back to keeping my boobs to myself."

"It'll get better," Jessica says vaguely. What everyone says to a new mother.

So Tracy asks, "Do you think you'll have another one?" What everyone says to the mother of one child.

"I doubt it," Jessica says.

"You don't want to? Or David doesn't?"

"I don't know what he wants anymore."

Tracy looks at the trembling corner of Jessica's mouth with a sliver of hope. Maybe she can finally get something raw and real out of her sister again.

"It's a little weird, having Christmas," Jessica says finally. "You don't mind?"

"It's nothing: a bunch of presents, some chocolate Santa Clauses."

"You're not going to teach Alice to believe in Santa Claus, are you?"

"Jesus, Jess! You used to be a slut, not a stick-in-the-mud."

"Don't be mean to me, please." Jessica's face crumples, her heavily lined eyes welling up.

"I'm sorry, I was joking."

"Everything's falling apart."

"What's going on?"

"I don't want to discuss the details right now."

But the details are everything, as Tracy's constantly reminding the high school students in her English classes. The details are what count. Without details, you can't expect people to care about anything you have to say.

Tracy switches Alice to the other side, grimacing at the baby's iron jaw. "Well, how's Ari doing? How do you handle relationship conflicts with a kid? I'm asking for my own future reference."

"You keep things as normal as possible," Jessica says defensively, case closed.

During their father's illness, Jessica handled things with

a managerial competence that Tracy was thankful for, but sometimes she'd wished her sister would ease up on the pious professionalism, that she'd talk about existential angst instead of estate planning, would just admit that the whole dying business was horrendous.

The hall closet at Jack and Tracy's overflows with coats and scarves, boots and hats, unmatched gloves and makeshift sleds. The refrigerator amasses an unsavory collection of leftovers. Only Francine, mother of two grown men, Jack and Barrett, seems to feel the responsibility to keep things orderly, including herself. Every morning in the hotel room she applies her full complement of makeup while Nicholas watches something unpleasant—a political talk show, a WWII documentary— with the volume turned up too loud. Francine believes people, especially women, should maintain themselves, preserve their dignity. Christina and Luke don't call her Grandma or any of the other silly old-lady names, but by her own given name. When Alice can talk, she will do the same. Francine finds it embarrassing the way Ruth babies her grandson, Ari, and frankly disappointing the way she mopes. It must be terribly difficult to lose one's husband, but Francine knows plenty of women who have, and after a time they've increased their volunteer work, planned trips with friends, signed up for extension classes at the nearby university.

At Jack and Tracy's, where the floor is always cluttered with toys and the coffee is never hot enough, Francine does what she can. She putters around, straightening books on the bookshelves, returning the perpetually left-out milk carton to the fridge. Being the mother of two boys, she should have become inured to messes long ago, but she could never quite get used to the chaos, the constant interruption and upheaval. Her life for years now has been calm, tastefully unhappy. She and Nicholas don't fight the way they used to, when the boys were still at home— about parenting, and their own parents, and even money, though they had plenty of it. They mixed drinks at the bar in the basement late at night and then laid into each other, his extroverted, combative personality up against her sneakier anger. It was a kind of sport; it made her strong. When she bathed afterward, by candlelight, in their beautiful marbled bathroom, she imagined leaving everyone behind and going to live in a nearly empty old farmhouse in the country: just a sturdy kitchen table, a well-made bed, and a stone fireplace, like her grandparents had. She scrubbed herself clean; she blazed with the desire to uproot everything. But now she and Nicholas are older than her grandparents were when they died; and he's had several heart surgeries; and their calendar is full: with charity events, and season tickets to the symphony and theater, and travel to the nice places one should see before one dies. After all these years, instead of arguing, Nicholas turns on the TV and Francine goes to bed early. She spreads the lavender satin eye pillow over her eyes, listens to the way the silence in the room isn't really silence. The most soundproof place in the world is actually right there in Minneapolis, in the city where she lives, a chamber built into a laboratory, where you can hear the loud thump of your own heartbeat. You have to stay seated in that room, she read in the newspaper. Otherwise you'll get dizzy and lose your balance in the absence of exterior sound cues, in the utterly disorienting chamber of your own body.

For a year now, Francine has had a secret. A childhood friend of hers named Raymond, whom she hasn't seen since high school, got in touch with her last Christmas, and they began emailing, then talking on the phone: long, warm, flirty conversations about everything and nothing. Raymond has lived alone in the South of France since his wife died five years ago, and he wants Francine to come visit. "Or you could just move in," he said last week, before she left for Ohio. "There's plenty of room. And a view of the sea. Water blue as your eyes. I remember how blue they are." He knows, of course, that she's married, that his proposal is absurd. Still, as if there's some understanding between them, he says *Je t'aime* at the end of their conversations, and she laughs that such foolish romance, such clandestine lightness, can exist in the world. It gives her something to think about at times when she feels utterly outside of life, standing here for instance, in her younger son's ramshackle house, wiping up the dining room table that everyone has scattered with brownie crumbs.

They're running out of food, and Tracy had planned on going to the grocery store herself. What was once a chore has become, since Alice's birth, an hour of escape. But Ruth insisted on coming along, and now, as they fill the cart to capacity (the benefit of this accompanied shopping trip is that her mother will pay), Ruth grills Tracy. How is she feeling, physically and mentally? Is she drinking enough fluids? Is she experiencing postpartum depression?

It's always been Ruth's way to introduce sensitive topics in public, as if she's specifically stored them up for a time when a retreat to one's private bedroom is impossible. In department store fitting rooms, customer service lines, and waiting rooms at doctors' offices, Tracy has endured questions about her friends, her love life, her diet, her personal relationship with Judaism.

"How's Jack adjusting to the baby?" Ruth asks, while they're waiting for sliced cheese at the deli counter. "Is he giving you the support you need?"

Tracy hesitates. It's her policy never to criticize Jack in front of her mother or to suggest any argument between the two of them. With his non-Jewishness already a strike against him, she doesn't want to provide anything further for Ruth to file away under some banal category: *shortcomings of my second son-in-law.* And yet Tracy is feeling frustrated. She has some sympathy for Jack, certainly, having to drag himself to school every weekday morning and impersonate a lively, quick-on-his-feet teacher, instead of a dazed new dad. On occasional nights he's up at whatever hour, feeding Alice from the precious stash of pumped milk, tending to her diaper. Most nights he moans like a man from whom the world is asking too much, pulls the covers over his head, and leaves Tracy to it. At least he hasn't retreated to sleep in a different room, like other new fathers they know, though whether that's out of loyalty to Tracy and Alice or devotion to the memory-foam mattress in their bedroom is up for debate. But she can feel their roles calcifying: the domestic tasks falling in her court, perhaps glomming on to her forever, like pregnancy pounds that can never be shed.

Tracy grabs a plastic container and begins packing it with olives. "He's really sweet with Alice," she says. "But I don't think he gets how much work it all is. I mean, this is what happens, right? The second shift and all that? Of course I'm not teaching now, but I'm afraid when I go back to it—"

For a moment Tracy thinks maybe they could have a conversation, woman to woman, about gender and societal norms, the bigger picture of family life and its injustices. Her mother had raised two kids while working a full-time job, with an overworked husband who never cooked a meal in his life. But Ruth's critique is grounded on the local level, directed at Jack's family.

"Well, he certainly doesn't have the greatest role model. Did you hear Nicholas this morning, kvetching about having to wait on hold to get a better room at some resort they're going to? What else does he have to do with his time? And then he asks Francine where his pills are and makes her drive back to the hotel to get them. *His* pills.

Not that she says a word about it. Just gets her fur coat and goes with that blank look."

The deli clerk hands them their cheese, and they wheel the cart over to the bakery aisle. Tracy wants it all. She wants all of the rich baked goods a breastfeeding woman deserves. She grabs an apple pie and a loaf of chocolate chip pumpkin bread. Her mother, who has a history of commenting on her weight, will not say anything today, when they're shopping for a houseful of people.

But Ruth's criticism of her in-laws feels like criticism of Tracy herself, by association. Ruth may be right, but Tracy suddenly feels defensive, especially of Francine, whom she believes, or wants to believe, feels things more deeply than she lets on. Jessica is fair game, though. Any sisterly allegiance they once had has been stripped away by Jessica's refusal to confide in Tracy for real. "Do you think Jess and David are okay?" Tracy ventures. "She sounded kind of down the other day about how things are going."

Ruth waves the concern away with a dismissive hand that comes back up with a box of molasses cookies. "It is what it is. It's just life, being married. Listen, this is what I told Jessica, and I'll say it to you too. If you're not getting along with your husband, if you're not feeling satisfied, just remember that one day he'll be dead and none of it will matter."

They pass the time in various familial configurations of walks around the neighborhood, sledding in the park, board games, kitchen duty, and sitting around. There's checkers, Monopoly, Pictionary, Boggle. There's looking at phones, and YouTube videos, and broken things in the house that Barrett attempts to fix, and Alice's darling face. There's talk of snow, snow tires, summer vacation plans, cell phone plans, things you can do with kale, political scandals, magic tricks, the tricks behind magic tricks, the complaint that there's nothing to do here, and the observation that children who say there's nothing to do must be dull people to think that. Each day is divided into periods of eating and not eating. Each person is divided into the public self they cultivate or let slip, and the private self they're afraid to reveal.

"Who's made New Year's resolutions?" Nicholas wants to know. "Who's ready to become a better person next year?"

"We're all joining the gym," Barrett says. "Family membership. Right, Chris?"

Christina scowls. Her dad knows she hates exercise, sports, anything that calls attention to her body. Her weight-loss plan involves making herself throw up like her friend Mia does. She hasn't worked up the nerve yet, but in the New Year she's resolved to do it.

"I'm gonna start taking judo classes," Luke says. "Kick some butt." In the fantasies he spends a lot of time playing out in his head, the terrorists storm James Madison Middle School, and he crushes them—part physical trouncing, part mental outsmarting.

"Who else?" Nicholas bellows. "Jessica? David?"

Jessica is working on a puzzle with Ari at the dining room table: the solar system in two hundred pieces. "Decluttering," she says. "We should only have what we need and give everything else away."

"People don't need our junk," David says from behind the newspaper. "If we really want to help people, we should volunteer our time. That's what I'm going to do."

Jessica pounds Mars into place.

"Noble pursuits," Nicholas says. "Now how will you all stick to them? Every year my wife resolves to bring me breakfast in bed, but does she do it?"

"Don't listen to him," Francine says.

I'm not, Ruth thinks. She's had enough of his bluster. Why does he get to be alive when her husband is buried in Mount Zion Cemetery? She looks up at Nicholas, into the face that must have been handsome once and that still shines with arrogance. "What about you? How do you plan to improve yourself?"

"Do I need improving? I see you think I do." He laughs. "What would you suggest?"

"If you don't know, I can't tell you."

Nicholas laughs again, the sort of ready laugh deployed as a shield to deflect any arrow of criticism. He turns to Barrett and strikes up a conversation about golf.

Francine hasn't been asked what her New Year's resolutions are, and in that moment she makes one. Somehow, she will see Raymond this year. Fly to France, sit down across a table from him, look into his eyes, and listen to the voice inside herself that will say she is either crazy for going there, or crazy to go back home.

Colorful foil horns and takeout Chinese food, pale ale and Pepto-Bismol. The indignity of not having a TV in the house on New Year's Eve has been remedied by David, who's unplugged the neighbors' nineteen-inch Panasonic and carried it over to Jack and Tracy's, set it up in a place of honor in the living room. Jack wants to object—*Leave Alan and Betty's TV alone!*—but he feels powerless to affect the sway of stupid tradition. Now everyone can watch the ball descend into Times Square, people screaming for no reason, for the one-digit change in the Gregorian calendar. Let everyone do what everyone does on New Year's Eve: same old, same old.

Barrett and Michelle sit shoulder to shoulder on the couch, chatting about the celebrities at the onscreen bash. In separate corners on the floor, Christina and Luke text furiously. Ari rests against Jessica, determined to stay up until midnight. And Alice is awake again, for her late-night bout of crankiness. Jack carries her into the kitchen, where Francine is loading the dishwasher. "Mom, you don't have to do that," he says.

"Who will do it then?" she protests. She touches Alice's cheek, the shocking softness. "Do you ever talk to Claire?"

His mother's question surprises Jack. They haven't

mentioned his ex-wife since he started seeing Tracy, back before the divorce was finalized.

"No. It was a pretty clean break. What made you think of her?"

"I was just thinking that it took courage to start over again like you did," Francine says. "New job. New wife."

Jack laughs. "When you put it that way, it sounds callous. I don't know that I'm brave. Maybe I just didn't try hard enough." Alice squawks, and he flies into motion. "She wants me to keep moving." He begins swinging her: toward Francine, then toward the refrigerator; Francine-bound, then fridgeward again.

When Alice was born, he did think of Claire. During their last big fight, before they settled into the cold, final certainty of separation, she'd screamed about wanting to have a baby with him, how she might never have one now. He hopes that won't turn out to be true.

"It's time!" Michelle calls from the living room. "Francine! Jack!" And they're drawn to the TV, to the countdown, like everyone else. "Ten-nine-eight-seven-six-five-four-three-two-one." As if the New Year is a space shuttle about to blast them into a different zone of being. Only for Alice, Jack thinks. Only she will change that much in one year.

"Let's toast," Barrett says, pouring champagne for the adults, Martinelli's cider for the kids. "To the newest member of this great extended family. To Alice Keeling!"

Jack notices Ruth flinch, as if her granddaughter's full

name hurts her. Tracy had suggested once, near the end of her pregnancy, that they might give their daughter her own last name, her dead father's name. But Jack didn't want to do that. Tracy carried their child in her body, was going to give birth to her. Let his daughter have his name at least. It's another thing to feel guilty for now, to wonder about whether it might be held against him.

Everyone clinks glasses, sips quietly, as the TV people rock out their glee.

"Right now," Luke says. "Now the psycho killer's gonna break down the door and shoot us."

"What are you talking about?" Christina shrieks.

"That's when it always happens," Luke says. "When everybody's happy and celebrating and not thinking they're going to die."

Around 12:30, when the party breaks up, Jack and Tracy dress for bed the way they do now, since the baby. They used to sleep naked, had declared to each other, a kind of private marriage vow, that they always would. But if you have to get up multiple times on a cold winter night, it turns out it's best to be fully clad in flannel pajamas and wool socks. They kiss chastely and say goodnight, then roll their separate ways in bed. A few hours later Alice awakens, bleats for milk. Tracy brings her into bed, glancing at the clock radio with its glowing announcement of the hour: 3:27. A friend had told her that when the baby woke you in the middle of the night, it was best not to look at the time, that it just made you feel more exhausted to know. But Tracy can't not look. One day at school last year, when she returned to her classroom after lunch, she found that some prankster had covered up the clock face with a homemade sign: *Time Does Not Exist.* She kept it up for the rest of the day as a philosophy lesson, but it drove her crazy; she gave herself an F.

Jack stirs and strokes Tracy's arm, and she sighs, flinching at the tug of Alice's unforgiving mouth. "Why did we do this?"

"You mean have a baby? Or let everyone come here?"

"Both, I guess. But at least she's cute," Tracy says.

"Yeah, imagine if we'd had an ugly baby."

"Do you think we'd even recognize it? Maybe she's not really that cute."

"No, she's very, objectively, cute." Jack's still stroking Tracy's arm and then gripping her wrist tight, and she's hit with a charge she hasn't felt since before Alice was born: the effect his body can have on her body.

"I just keep stupidly hoping they'll turn into people I can actually talk to," she says.

"Nope. They'll keep on being a bunch of sourpuss Jews."

Tracy pulls her arm away. "Well your family's a bunch of oblivious WASPs."

"Hey, joke. It was a joke."

"You're as funny as your dad."

Alice's sucking has stopped, her eyes shut up tight. Tracy lays her back down in the bassinet. In the baby's long white sleep sack, she looks like the angel that's missing from the top of their Christmas tree. Is it wrong to feel the most affection for her at this moment, when she's absent from the sentient world, in need of nothing and no one? Back in bed, Jack's body gives off heat.

Tracy could press against him, draw that heat into herself. Enough time has passed; the bleeding ended weeks ago. Instead she lies still, thinking of her father, who kept in touch with all of his relatives, even the ones he didn't seem to like much. The concept of family was important to him in a way that had always seemed suspect to Tracy. So they were people who shared your name, your genes, whatever. Wasn't that whole blood-is-thicker-than-water thing a relic, really, from a time when bloodlines were used to keep peasants confined to their class, to justify slavery and segregation, to murder Jews in ovens? Still, there was something charming about her father's belief that Tracy might care when he reported that so-and-so distant cousin, whom she couldn't remember ever meeting, had had a baby. Now he will never know that it happened to Tracy too, that she has a little daughter, like he'd had once.

Tomorrow, everyone will leave. She and Jack have made it through their first holiday season as parents. Alice has met her three surviving grandparents, her aunts and uncles, her cousins. Everyone has held her, even six-year-old Ari. If there is anything to be agreed upon, it's that Alice is adorable, precious. And she has no context for understanding how much affection her family has lavished on her. No awareness that she may grow up to feel estranged from them all.

January third, a date steeped in doom. It ends here: the winter vacation that had seemed so long and luxurious at the start. Jack hurries out the door at dawn to scrape ice and snow off the car, to prepare for students as unenthused as he is to be back at school. Tracy is taking this whole year off, a privilege they had planned for, saved for, but hearing Jack's car start up while she sits on the couch with Alice, she wishes that she were going with him. She misses talking about books, misses those kindred-spirit students who find reading to be a lifeline. If only she had a nanny, or better yet, a mother nearby—not hers, certainly, but one like her friend Raka's mother, wonderfully sane and thoroughly capable, who would come over during the day and take care of the baby for free.

It'll go by so fast, both Ruth and Francine had said to Tracy, as if they were confiding some profound insight, some realization about parenting that had never been voiced before. *Enjoy it.* As much a rebuke, perhaps, as a blessing. Okay, so they're getting to be old women, they have the right to be wistful about the passage of time, to romanticize the early years of their practically middle-aged adult children, children who worshipped them once, when small enough to be blinded by love. But time doesn't feel fast to Tracy. It feels slow as snow falling.

"I'm your mother," she says aloud to Alice. "Isn't that strange? What do you think of me? I mean, be honest."

It's quiet but for the rush of the furnace shuttling into gear. They live off the main road, away from traffic. The neighbors who keep pets have stealthy cats, nary a barking dog on the street. The mail carrier doesn't come by till late afternoon. Tracy sets the baby down on the couch, where, being too young to do anything but flutter her hands and feet, she will stay put.

Alice looks up—not a blank look, not a dumb look. In just these two weeks, her vision has sharpened. Colors have come in. The crimson of her mother's loungewear, the navy of the couch cushions. And distance, too, a recognition of how matter aligns itself in air. The branches of the Christmas tree standing in the corner of the living room have assumed a branchlike structure, definition instead of blur. Alice can focus her eyes and track the movement of objects. She can see the strings of lights, descending from the tree now and disappearing into a box. The front door opens to whiteness, a blast of cold. The tree moves farther and farther away until it's out of sight. For a moment she's alone. Where to look? Where to look?

And then, ah—there it is. That face, returning. The most familiar thing, and still for now, for that reason, the most interesting thing, the most pleasing thing. She looks and looks as if she can't get enough, as if her mother's face tells her everything she wants to know.

A Lady Who Takes Jokes

When Kamal's eight-year-old daughter Laila wants to know what my job is, I tell her I spend my days trying to make babies laugh.

"That's the easiest job I ever heard of," Laila says. "You just give them a zerbert on the belly."

"That would do it," I admit. "We can't touch them, though."

"Are they sick?" Laila looks worried.

"No, not at all. Our study examines how babies respond to things they see and hear. So physical touch—things like zerberts and tickling—that's cheating."

From her perch next to me on the couch, Laila sets her chin in her hand and regards me with Kamal's hard-driving green eyes. Most kids I've known haven't bothered to ask what I'm doing with my life. But Laila takes an interest. As the first woman her dad's dated since his divorce, I expected her to resent me. Instead, she seems ready to count me as a friend—that is, if I prove to be worthy.

"Can they watch funny cartoons?" she asks.

"We do show them videos, actually, but the babies are so little they don't quite know what's funny yet. They learn to laugh from their interactions with people. We're trying to understand how we—humans, I mean—learn about funniness."

"I wonder what my dad's doing in there." Laila jumps up and runs into the kitchen.

It's not the first time I've gotten that sort of reaction when attempting to explain what I study. As E. B. White famously said, analyzing humor is like dissecting a frog. The poor frog, the poor joke.

Kamal's living room couch is silky and cream-colored, woven with tapestry flowers. Opposite the couch, there's a curio cabinet filled with clay beads, gold rings, pieces of pottery, and sea glass. On our first date, when Kamal brought me back to his house, he told me they were centuries-old artifacts discovered across Lebanon. I wasn't sure at first if he was telling the truth. Irony seemed to be lying in wait behind his velvety voice.

"How did you get them?" I asked warily.

"My parents," he said, as if it were obvious, as if everyone's parents give their children ancient treasures.

"And how did they get them?"

"They're archaeologists. After the strikes in Beirut in '06, they gave this collection to me for safety. They think nothing will happen in Seattle."

The big earthquake is coming, the seismologists warn, the worst natural disaster in North American history.

There's a one-in-three chance it will happen in the next fifty years. But an earthquake is a grand abstraction. Generally, the tepid rain falls and we Seattleites sip our lattes in peace.

Kamal emerges from the kitchen with a platter of flatbread brushed with olive oil and spices, which he calls a thyme pizza. He sets it down on the dining room table and hands me another cappuccino with perfect foam. Laila climbs into the chair across from mine.

"Did you never have a thyme pizza before?" she asks.

"Nope. This is my first." I take a bite while she watches. "Delicious." Compared to this complex blend of flavors, American pizza is a cheesy embarrassment.

"My mom says the minute you taste my dad's food you forgive him for everything."

"Laila," Kamal warns. A native speaker of both Arabic and French, he pronounces his daughter's name beautifully—Lah-ay-lah, the Ls lilting off the tongue. "Go get some labneh for Caitlin."

What did he need to be forgiven for? He's kind, conscientious, tidy. Over the past few months, I've learned it's not irony in his voice after all, but sincerity balanced with well-considered restraint. His laugh is almost noiseless. He angles his head back, bares his slightly crooked, non-American teeth.

When Laila disappears into the kitchen, I tease him about her gibe, but I can't get anything out of him.

"She was just joking," he says.

"It's the sad truth," I say, "that most jokes aren't that funny."

My friend Lucy is the one with the funniest jokes, the one who gets it—me, everything—the most. She lives on the East Coast, where I grew up, three time zones away. We talk late at night, after her husband's gone to sleep, and though there's no one else in my apartment to hear what I'm saying, I close the door to my bedroom and turn off the light. We've known each other since we were fifteen, when our parents sent us off to summer camp. Eight weeks of sports in the blistering sun, ugly arts-and-crafts projects, rubbery hot dogs, peanut butter on flaccid bread, poison ivy, mosquito bites, catty girls saying foolish things about boys. That is to say, it was like most summer camps, but we weren't the summer-camp kind. Having identified each other as outcasts from across bunk lines, we spent as much time together as possible. Just between the two of us, we made concentration camp jokes. "Don't go in the shower," we warned each other after instructional swim. And when the tyrannical senior girls' counselor barked orders: "Watch out for Eva Braun." We felt it was our right to say things like this, having suffered through years of Hebrew school. During our free period we read aloud from *The Handmaid's Tale,* scratched "Don't let the bastards grind you down" into a tree. At dances we stuck by the refreshments table, eating too many Doritos and half-heartedly mocking the music. People assumed we were lesbians. "Do you guys, like, listen to Melissa Etheridge a lot?" they sneered.

After dinner, while the other girls did one another's makeup; made fun of the older, unattractive counselors; and ranked the hotness of TV stars, we escaped to the canteen, and Lucy entertained me with jabs at our bunkmates.

"Why is a white girl like a tampon?"

"Why?"

"They're both stuck up cunts."

"*We're* white," I said, shocked and delighted.

"Jewish. We get a pass."

Now Lucy has a baby named Arthur. I flew out to meet him right before I started dating Kamal. Arthur was five weeks old then. He had a crazy lot of dark hair and a quizzical expression. He made bleeps and bloops with his little baby lips. He shook his hands in the air when he was sleeping, as if he were conducting an imaginary orchestra.

"Are all babies this funny?" Lucy asked. Because I work with babies, she considers me an expert.

"Nope," I said. "This one is a rare comic genius."

It was strange to see my best friend graduated to this stage of responsibility and care. Holding and feeding Arthur, Lucy said she felt like she was just playing being a mother, but then that was our attitude toward life: that you spend most of your time fumbling around in your roles, and only occasionally do you really feel like yourself. Her husband Josh had become dadlike, with a burp cloth tossed over his henley shirt; he seemed gentler and more mature than I'd seen him before. Together, they looked like Arthur's parents, each of them declaring they saw the other one in their son.

When Lucy and I talk on the phone now, Arthur's usually in the background: making grunting and sucking sounds, sometimes fussing to the point where we have to hang up. Lucy says she's so exhausted she falls asleep sitting at her desk at work. She says yes, this time is precious, but she can't wait for Arthur to be old enough to do something other than eat, poop, and cry. She says she's sorry she's turned into one of those women who can only talk about her kid.

I play the part of the spicy single friend, feeding her details about Kamal. I tell her that he's introduced me to my all-time favorite drink: Pernod and soda, served in a rose-colored crystal glass. I tell her that he smokes clove cigarettes that come in stylish yellow packages, and that kissing his musky mouth is actually better than kissing a nonsmoker whose breath tastes of mouthwash. I tell her about the way he speaks French with Laila, the two of them pooching their lips out and flicking their hands in the air.

Tonight, Lucy grumbles about a woman on the street who scolded her for having Arthur out without a hat. Then she asks, "How's Mr. Sexy, Exotic, and Rich?"

"He's not rich."

"Hmm. Clove cigarettes. French private school for his daughter."

"He has his priorities. And his job at Microsoft."

"Do you know what he does all day?"

"He's a computer programmer. So no, I have no idea."

"Well, enjoy him," she sighs. "Go out, drink, fuck. Don't smoke."

All through our twenties, Lucy and I traded stories of ridiculous dates, confusing sex, relationships going nowhere, breakups circling back into relationships going nowhere. Then she met Josh, and her jokes about becoming an old maid cat lady who hates cats turned into jokes about becoming a Jewish mother who neglects her children. For me, the subject of having my own family has become too serious to laugh at. I'll be thirty-six this year: almost beyond eligibility, or so society and my mom would have me believe.

"Kamal and I don't have enough in common, do we?"

"Enough for what? To end up with a baby on your boob while he snores in the basement?"

When she found Josh, got married, and then got pregnant, I felt a kind of loss. I've had to struggle to shake myself out of it, to steel myself against crude envy.

Ten more minutes," Kamal keeps saying from the desk in his home office, where he's staring at columns of computer code. I came over after I got home from the lab, but he's still working, as he often is, in this language I can't possibly understand, more obscure even than the French or Arabic he speaks.

"That's what he always says to me." Laila intercepts

my path back to the living room. She's wearing a giant Mariners T-shirt and a pair of slippers with satin roses.

"How do you get him to stop?"

"There's nothing you can do. You just have to wait."

"You should be preparing for bed," Kamal calls from his office.

Laila makes a face. "Want to see my room?"

I've never been invited in before. The Tintin poster on her closed door—the boy in his rippling trench coat, the dog in a happy dash—gives the impression that Laila is busy inside with secret and vital missions.

From floorboards to crown molding, the walls are covered with crazy makeshift wallpaper: pages from coloring books and calendars; postcards; valentines; shiny squares of wrapping paper; ads for clothes, and pet food, and Caribbean cruises.

"This is amazing," I tell her. "Did you do it all yourself?"

"My dad hung up the high ones."

"What does he think of it?"

"He says it's hideous, but it's my room."

I point to a picture of a chimp laughing, tacked right next to a toothpaste ad with a picture of a young woman baring her gleaming gums.

"I like this one."

"It's from *National Geographic.*"

"Did you know that primates laugh when they're tickled, just like we do?"

"Yeah, well that chimp is laughing because he played a trick on his friend."

"Really? What was the trick?"

"He stole his friend's banana and replaced it with a phone that looked like a banana. So the friend tried to eat it and the chimp thought it was really funny."

"Wow. Did the friend play a trick to get back at him?"

"No. They were just friends again."

Kamal knocks on the door and comes in before we can respond. "Are you holding Caitlin prisoner in your den? Go brush your teeth. And brush your hair or it'll be a mess tomorrow."

A lamp with a red shade glows amorously in Kamal's bedroom. The white-and-green patchwork quilt is embroidered with stars. If these are his recently divorced things, I wonder what his married things were like. A wooden cross hangs above the bed; he's a Maronite Christian. He kicks me out on Sunday mornings so he can attend services at the church he and his ex-wife have been going to since they came here from Lebanon. Nonetheless, I prefer to see the cross as a testament to his taste for lovely hand-carved objects, rather than as a religious symbol that means something to him. Hebrew school taught me that I'm an atheist.

Kamal emerges from the bathroom with a towel wrapped around his waist. I shower in the morning before I go out in public. He showers in the evening before our bodies touch. If I get into bed with clothes on, he scolds me: "You took the bus today. How many people do you think stick their asses in that seat every day?" So I'm naked under the covers now, waiting for him. At first the rule was no sex if Laila was in the house. Then it was reduced to no staying over on nights when she slept at Kamal's. But we broke that too.

Kamal climbs on top of the bed with his towel still in place. Water drips off the hair on his chest; his neck smells like oranges. He pulls back the quilt. "Nice," he says gruffly.

While he starts touching me, I ask, "Did you and Mariam ever think about having another kid?"

"Sure, we're both from big families. An only child is trouble, right?"

This is friendly teasing aimed at my own only-child status, which I ignore, because I'm testing how far I can dip into the treacherous waters of the past and the future.

"So why didn't you, then?"

"Well, we wanted to wait until Laila was older, and then by that time, we were fighting a lot."

"What were you fighting about?"

He tightens his grip on my thigh. "Why do you like to make me rehash it all? She thought I worked too much. I'm sure I did. She's unhappy with a lot of things in this country that I don't love either, but we've decided to be here, so what can we do? She accused me of turning into an entitled American. In the end, we just couldn't communicate."

Not for the first time, I think that I would like to meet Mariam, that she and I would have a lot to talk about.

"Would you still want another kid someday?" I stare up

at the ceiling as if this is a disinterested question, me his accidental naked shrink.

"I don't know," he says. "Maybe I'm resigned to Laila being an only child. You didn't turn out so bad."

Kamal's art of deflection is a polished one. He slides his hands over my stomach, my hip bones. He kisses my pubic hair. "We have to be quiet," he whispers.

"Okay," I whisper back, undoing his towel. The idea of making love covertly so that Laila can't hear us is erotic to me. But then Kamal is always quiet, his brow slightly crinkled, his lips slightly open, as if to admit a slim cigarette. I am the one who has to gasp into the pillow, suck the screams back inside my mouth.

Because I'm on the pill, my eggs stay put inside my ovaries. My fallopian tubes never see any action. It's a hoax, on a chemical level. The hormones in the pills convince the ovaries that ovulation has already taken place, that the monthly to-do list is done. Ha ha.

The next morning, while Kamal gets dressed, Laila and I drink our milk and eat the crepes he's prepared for us with Nutella and banana. She's finishing up a drawing of her family tree for school. The names are written inside birds' nests perched on the branches. At the bottom she's drawn a scrawny robin to represent herself.

"So most of your relatives are still in Lebanon, right?"

"We see them in the summer."

"They must be so glad when you come to visit."

"Yeah, they are."

I love her frankness, her lack of need for any false humility.

"Where does your family live?" Laila asks me.

"My parents are in New Jersey where I grew up. I visit them a few times a year."

"They're not divorced, are they?"

I want to lie and tell her that they are so this can be a bond between us.

"They're still together. But honestly, I don't think that's a good thing. Some parents stay married but it doesn't mean they're happy. When I was younger, I used to wish they'd get divorced."

"When I was younger, I wished mine would get back together."

Kamal and Mariam have been divorced for less than a year. Younger, to Laila, must mean seven instead of eight.

"What about now?"

"I know they won't." Laila shrugs. She picks up her colored pencil and draws a branch extending out from the nest that says *Kamal, Mon Père*. On the branch she writes my name—*Caitlin, Mon Amie*.

Most days at work I see babies. Babies flashing brilliant grins or dissolving into tears for no apparent reason. Babies looking clueless or in the know.

Their mothers bring them in—it's almost all mothers—wearing fancy slings, fully stocked diaper bags at the ready. What I told Laila isn't quite true: that my job is to make babies laugh. I'm more like the curator of their laughter, collecting it as specimens for study and analysis. Parents keep logs of when their babies laugh and what precedes the laughter. They record notes about situations in which the babies seem to be joking around with others. Every month they bring the logs in to me and respond to a questionnaire. For their part, the babies play for a bit, getting comfortable in the lab, and then they watch videos of people laughing in response to various stimuli. While a baby is looking at the screen, the eye tracker records his eye movements, indicating the duration and point of the gaze. This is the gold standard for infant research: where and for how long does the subject look? We can't have them fill out a survey. We can't give them tasks to perform. All we can do is look at them looking. When do they stare intently at the incongruous thing, the mischievous thing, the thing that doesn't fit with how people and objects are supposed to behave? When do they look away, tired of the same old joke?

When Lucy calls at the wrong time—in the middle of the day—I'm sitting in my office between appointments, so I pick up the phone. Her sobs are terrible adult sobs, her choked-out words impossible. The day before yesterday, she'd put Arthur to bed. Everything seemed fine. But in the morning, she woke to silence instead of his siren cry. She rushed to his room and he wasn't breathing. The paramedics came; they couldn't revive him. He died. Her baby died.

There have been times, over the twenty years of our friendship, when, I'm ashamed to admit, I've enjoyed listening to her cry, have welcomed being chosen as the one to receive her pain. Have felt less alone because she's unhappy too. But this is something entirely different, this wipes out anything we might have imagined to be sorrow. Having given me the news, gotten out the words that must be the hardest words to say, Lucy whispers that she has to go and hangs up.

My office is strewn with toys I need to tidy before the next subject arrives: musical balls, rainbow-colored rattles, stuffed animals with stitched-on smiles. I picture Lucy opening the door to Arthur's room and hurrying over to the crib. I remember the way he looked—weirdly wise beyond his years, his months—when I'd told Lucy that he was a comic genius.

I could round up a lab assistant to take over for the rest of the day, but I don't want to have to tell my coworkers what happened, and I don't want to leave our psych-lab haven. Here, we live in the land of laughing babies. We chart their month-by-month progress: the increasing deftness of their limbs, the evidence of their developing brains. We believe that playfulness is all. I wipe my eyes and blow my nose and open my office door for the next mother and baby.

At first it's a relief that Laila is at her mother's house for a few days. Kamal settles me on the couch with a blanket over my legs, brings me a bowl of lentil soup. "What exactly happened to the baby?" he asks.

"One of those inexplicable things, I guess. SIDS. For lack of a better diagnosis."

"What a nightmare." He shakes his head. "There will be a funeral?"

"Yeah, on Sunday."

"You'll fly out?"

I hesitate before answering. I know he won't approve; he shouldn't approve. "I don't think so," I tell him.

"But she's your best friend."

"She'll have her family with her. I don't think it would really help for me to be there."

This, I know, is not the point. The point is, a horrible thing has happened to Lucy, and I'm too terrified to face it.

"Okay," Kamal says, in his I'm-not-going-to-push-it voice. "You need a distraction. Let's watch a movie."

The movie is in French, beautifully boring, with subtitles that sound more formal than the way people really talk. I keep closing my eyes, and when I open them again, it doesn't seem that I've missed anything. When Kamal falls asleep next to me, I wish we'd spent the evening with Laila around instead, that we'd had her to focus on. I would have had to tell her, to explain why I was sad. And she would take it like kids her age do: the evidence of their thoughtfulness alive on their faces. It would trouble her, not in the way such a thing troubles an adult, shuddering at the loss of a mother's child, but in an almost philosophical way, trying to grasp that the world is capable of such a thing. And I could have pretended that by talking about it with Laila, I was being an honorable grown-up.

On Sunday, while Kamal is at church and Lucy is burying her four-month-old baby, I take the bus into downtown Seattle and walk along the waterfront. The gray-green water ruffles up, white-capped and choppy. The giant ferryboat trolls its perpetual route across Puget Sound. Tourists buy cheap replicas of the Space Needle that fit neatly in the hand. The rain holds off.

When I settled on a psychology major in college, I decided early on that I didn't want to do clinical. I didn't want to become a therapist. No fifty-minute hour for me. No borderline personality disorder, no chemical dependency, no couples struggling with their marriages, no razor blades to the wrist. I'm a good-enough listener, if listening means knowing the right questions to ask to get people to open up, the nonjudgmental murmurings to encourage them to continue speaking. I've been told that I have an approachable, sympathetic face. But I don't, in my heart, feel I have the power to help people. And it turns out that I'm a coward. I'm afraid to see what Arthur's death has done to Lucy's face.

A few times I speak to the voice on her voicemail, her former voice: pleasant, professional, untouched by grief. "I'm just calling to say hi," I tell her. "You don't have to call me back. I love you." I've never been one to throw the word *love* around. Now I'm hoping it possesses magical properties.

One night Laila asks me to tell her a bedtime story. For a moment I panic. I'm not sure I know any stories. I kneel beside her fairy-tale bed, all lavender and lace. Under the covers, with her long hair shimmering from static electricity, she looks like a princess, safeguarded from the world. Kamal, sitting at the foot of the bed in his violet and gold bathrobe, looks like an emperor awaiting the evening entertainment. I stare at Lucy's wall, at the picture of the beaming chimp.

"Okay, so once upon a time, there was a chimp," I manage to begin. "He was known throughout the forest for his crazy laugh." I describe the forest: sturdy vines for swinging, bananas hanging from every other tree, high perches that serve as lookouts for lions and hunters.

"What was the chimp's name?" Lucy interrupts.

"Arthur. His name was Arthur. He laughed all the time. He couldn't stop laughing, which was weird, because the things that were happening in his life were sad."

I describe his misfortunes: his favorite tree gets chopped down; a sister goes missing; the bananas he plucks turn into phones, with zookeepers calling and making threats. Arthur keeps laughing his wild laugh. The other chimps get annoyed. *What's wrong with you?* they complain. *This really isn't funny.* But Arthur can't help it. He gets these attacks of the giggles, the way you do when you're at school or church, someplace where you're not supposed to laugh, and that makes you laugh even more.

Finally, he laughs so hard he starts crying, and then he's crying for real. He cries all night, while the rest of the forest sleeps: the sloths hanging upside down from branches, the birds with one eye open, the other chimps cuddled together in their nests. In the morning, his tears have made a river, and the river brings his sister back, on a boat made out of the trunk of his favorite tree.

"The end," I say.

There is silence, the kind of silence that makes me aware of each individual brain as an organ that no one but its owner has access to, an organ that will shut down forever after five minutes without oxygen.

"Sad," Kamal says, eyeing me with his beautiful, serious face.

"The ending's happy," Laila says. "I like Arthur. Are there other stories about him?"

"Another night," Kamal says.

"Another night," I say.

Today's baby, nine months old, is named Lionel. His mother's name is Felicia. They're both cute and sprightly, sun-haired and moon-faced. This is their fourth visit. Each month Felicia turns in her typed-up notes about Lionel's laughter history. They're a data collector's dream, clear and detailed in the right ways, free of the kind of sentimental excess that tells us more about the writer than the subject.

Felicia sets Lionel down on the rug and he wriggles toward the felt blocks, stuffs them in his mouth, topples over, and bops back up.

"What will you do with the data once you're done?" Felicia asks.

"Oh, we'll look for patterns. We'll think about our findings in relation to other studies on infant socialization. Then, if the results seem significant, we'll try to publish an article."

"Great," Felicia says.

If she questions the importance of such research, she is right in doing so. In our grant proposals we attempt to make the case that by studying what causes laughter in infants, we can better understand human socio-cognitive development. But I know we're not saving any lives here.

Lionel keeps trying to bite my shoe. I'm not sure if it's my responsibility to try to stop him, if shoes are too unsanitary for mouthing, or if it's one of those things where you decide as a parent, oh what the hell. Felicia makes no move to stop it. "I know you're probably not supposed to say, but have you noticed anything about Lionel in particular, in relation to other babies?"

What is it she wants to hear? That he's on par, that he's normal, or that he's a superstar? I praise Lionel's attention span, his responsive and adaptable nature, and Felicia appears satisfied. Now she can confirm what she already knows: that her baby is perfect.

Though I study babies, I've never actually been much of a "baby person." When I think that I want a kid, I mean a kid. Someone old enough to tend to her own basic hygiene, to understand that her mother isn't an extension of herself, to know why some things are interesting and others are dumb. But still young enough to be sweet, to think bedtime requires stories, to fail to get the joke because she hasn't yet learned enough about meanness. Lately, though, I've seen babies that have made me think, okay, I'd take that one. Babies charged with the life force: waggling their butts as they rev up to crawl and hissing good-naturedly, as if to propose that everything is just a game, everything is for fun.

When Lucy finally calls me back, I'm about to pull into Kamal's driveway. "Hold on a minute," I tell her, and park facing a stand of spruce trees. One of the branches is turned up in such a way that it looks like it's giving me the finger.

"There's something I need to say," Lucy says, when I come back on the phone.

"Of course." I wait for her to lay into me, to tell me I'm a shitty friend for not showing up to her child's funeral.

She starts crying. "Fuck, I'm so tired of crying."

Up on the second floor of Kamal's house, the curtains

part slightly and Laila peeks out. I wave, give her a half smile.

"Only Josh knows this. And the medical examiner." She gets her voice under control and begins speaking with the flatness of a confession: words she's rehearsed for some jury, for me. "He had such a hard time staying asleep. I told you that. He flailed around in his crib. Even when we swaddled him, he'd burst out of the blanket. So a week or so before he—I started putting him down on his stomach. He slept better that way."

"Okay," I say, to encourage her to continue, and the composed voice is gone.

"No, it's not okay. Don't you know? You don't do that these days. *Back to sleep. Always put your baby down to sleep on his back.* So if he has some—I don't know—some breathing problem, something wrong with him for some unknown fucking reason, he's less likely to suffocate. I wanted him to sleep. And he never woke up."

Lucy is wailing so loudly now I think protectively of Laila, though of course from her second-floor perch, she couldn't possibly hear.

"But they're not faulting you, right? It's not illegal to put your baby down that way. People have done it for years, and their babies—you didn't cause his death, Luce."

She doesn't respond, but she's stopped sobbing, and so I keep talking, telling her in as many ways as I can think of that she cannot blame herself, that she must not, that I will not allow her to. This is why she's called, why she's saved this secret for me. Because she knows I'll deliver, that this is my wheelhouse—the thing that makes you feel just a tiny bit better about being your faulty self—and my voice gets stronger and stronger with relief over having something to talk about that isn't just the raw terrible truth of it, which matters beyond anything and which nothing will change.

When we hang up and I get out of the car, Laila opens the door before I can knock, and asks, "Who were you talking to?"

"My friend Lucy."

"Does she live in Seattle?"

"No, she's in Rhode Island. Far away."

Laila studies my face, and for a moment I wonder if Kamal said something to her. But no. There would have been no reason for him to do that.

"Do you want to hear a joke?" she asks.

"Sure."

"Why was the baby ant confused?"

"Why?"

"Because his ants were uncles. I mean, his uncles were ants."

"Good one," I say, laughing at her flub despite myself, despite the conversation in the car that weighs heavy on my chest.

"I messed it up."

"It's still funny, though."

"Papa's working. I'll go get him."

She zips off, and I think about stopping her, grasping her thin shoulders and peering straight into the eyes that look so much like her father's and yet are hers alone. *Actually, it's you. You're the one that I want.*

I'm not sure who will break up with whom and when, but I think it will be mutual. I think it will be soon. We'll be civil and tastefully sad—no hysterics, no dramatic declarations. Perhaps we'll have one final night of quiet sex. If I see Laila again, it will be only by accident: down the aisle of a Middle Eastern market in the International District, across the cavernous fountain at Seattle Center. There can be no custody arrangement between an ex-girlfriend and boyfriend and his child with another woman. No Wednesday evenings or Sunday afternoons together. Not even the lesser holidays: Columbus Day, Veterans Day, April Fools'.

When I was fifteen, though I'd spent eight weeks longing for that wretched summer camp to end, on the last day I was heartbroken. That I was no longer going to lock eyes with Lucy at breakfast every morning, while Eva Braun led the senior girls in a camp cheer. Or hang out at the canteen in the evening, drinking orange soda and popping Mike and Ikes, trying to soothe ourselves for not fitting in by critiquing everyone else. I was heartbroken that we lived in different states; that I wasn't sure she needed me as much as I needed her.

Our friendship survived. Still, I know how easily it could have gone the other way. If she hadn't been the one to call me first and ask, "What's the difference between a Jew and a pizza?" If she hadn't talked me through parents that didn't understand and relationships that fell apart, and taught me that humor can be what saves you. So that I could grow up to be a woman waiting for her to tell me a joke again and make me laugh—even after what she's suffered, even when I should be the one building the boat, setting out from the forest to find her, as fast as the river will carry me.

Love Bug, Sweetie Dear, Pumpkin Pie, Etc.

He called her by her name, Serena, only under certain circumstances. When they were about to be late for some event because she was still in front of the mirror, frowning at her hair. When she stewed over some small mistake she'd made. When she predicted a negative outcome instead of a more hopeful one.

Otherwise, he called her all of the things she used to wonder if she would ever be called when she was thirteen years old, shy and pimply, and falling asleep at night listening to 92.5 KISS FM on her headphones: *Honey. Darling. Sweetie. My love. My lover.* Sometimes he riffed on her name: *Serenita, serenade me.* Having studied in Argentina for a year in college, he had a repertoire of telenovela-style endearments for her too: *Mi vida. Mi corazón. Mi alma.* He was a big man with a carefully shaved face, who walked around the house singing Cole Porter tunes, '80s pop, and Puccini arias. He loved William Blake, Frank Lloyd Wright, Maurice Sendak, spaghetti carbonara, air-conditioning, and the smell of vanilla. As they stroked and sighed their way toward sex, he would murmur in her ear: *You, you, you, you.* The word transformed her; she became someone lovelier than herself. When their personality differences plunged them into dispute, the tension could lead to grim silence for days at a time. And then she would miss the familiar harmonies of his voice—relating bits from his constant reading, humming tunes from his repertoire of songs, buzzing the buzz of their lives together.

His name was Henry and Serena called him Henry. There'd been a time early on when she'd tested out a few pet names for him, but they sounded phony, like she was trying to be some other kind of softer, sweeter girlfriend— maybe one who enjoyed yoga, knitting, making soup—or like she was imitating him.

After they married she could present him to others as *my husband,* and that appealed to her categorical impulses. She worked as a research librarian at the nearby university. He was a freelance book designer, working from home in a studio in their attic. She paid for their health insurance. He drew funny pictures on the napkins that came with their takeout dinners. She liked sitting behind her desk at the library, surveying the vast, orderly collection before her. He liked holding the book manuscript in his hands, still coverless, waiting for him to fashion its one perfect dress.

They were going to be that couple who didn't have kids, who lived in a house free of soggy Cheerios on the floor and crayon marks on the wall, who could go out together spontaneously any night of the week. They were going to read thick classic novels and listen to the most inventive podcasts and travel frequently to foreign countries, serenely sipping their airplane cocktails above the clouds, while the inevitable children of other people squalled in another row. They were going to save well for retirement, and find doctors to prescribe medication they could use to kill themselves if it came to that, and die without leaving anyone except the rest of the world behind.

Then, when they were both thirty-seven, Henry started offering to hold babies, playing peek-a-boo with toddlers in restaurants. Serena often came home from work to find him next door, in the driveway of their neighbors' house, shooting baskets with the nine-year-old boy. They went to see one of those European movies about a gruff older man befriending a winsome child, and Henry kept wiping his eyes. One Saturday morning, when Serena was making a rare attempt at French toast, he came into the kitchen and swept his arms around her.

"Honey, I've changed my mind. I want to have a baby. With you."

"Not with Adrienne?" she teased, stalling for time. A divorced piano teacher, Adrienne lived down the street. The previous evening, at a neighborhood party, she kept swooping around Henry with her giant bosom and swirling hair, suggesting they make music together.

"She's forty-three. You're getting there, but you're not that old yet."

"I bet she could squeeze some milk out of those breasts."

"You still don't want to?" Disappointment made Henry handsome: his eyes greened, his lips plumped.

"We both didn't want to."

"People change. We could be the kind of parents we wished we had."

Serena concentrated on whisking the bright eggs into milk. Seeing her friends become mothers had only solidified her lack of interest in becoming one herself. She was content to be the pseudo aunt, to buy the children beautiful picture books and fancy cupcakes, spend a few hours in their self-absorbed company, and then drive home in her clean car. She didn't envy the interminable job her friends had taken on. The way they could never have an uninterrupted conversation when their kids were around. The way they complained about being so tired; the way they looked so tired. Even the occasional pleasure they seemed to take in their children—and sure, the kids were cute in ponytails or frog boots, and they said funny things sometimes—well, frankly, it embarrassed her. The exaggerated smooches on grubby cheeks. The crowing about some developmental achievement that, soon enough, would mean nothing at all. So the kid could eat solid food, walk, talk, recite the alphabet, pump his legs on a swing, memorize a Disney song. Who couldn't, sooner or later?

But now Henry was under the spell of that biological enchantment: to recombine DNA for the hundred billionth whatever time. And what would be the marital compromise? Have half a kid?

"Sit down," Serena said. She served them rubbery French toast and lukewarm coffee.

Henry wouldn't stop looking at her. "So you're completely set against this?"

"We should talk about it."

"Okay." He cut the French toast into four giant squares and drenched them in syrup. "Go ahead and talk."

"Why do you want a baby?"

"It might be fun. It could be amazing. I know I used to say I didn't feel the need to have kids, but that was probably just youth talking. Youth and fear. Now I'm getting old and sentimental."

"You were always sentimental."

"The other week, at Ed and Marta's, when Julien was crying? I took him outside to look at the birds, and I thought, why am I afraid I'd be like my dad? I'm not a cold person. Why would I be a bad father?"

"You wouldn't be," she said. "But having your own child isn't like entertaining a baby for an hour. It's all the time. It's constant."

"Hey, I'm not naïve. I know how much work it is. I know I don't even know how much work it is."

She could foresee how this would go: the back and forth that calcified into entrenched positions. People left each other for less. People lived for years, decades, with grand resentments lodged like icebergs under the surface of every petty fight. It would be on her head: that she'd claimed Henry's endearments for herself alone, prevented him from creating another human being upon whom to bestow them.

S he got pregnant within the first month of sex without a condom, when she was flooded with semen and panic. All these years, then, birth control really had served as a protective shield against spawning a gaggle of babies. Now her belly grew bulging and sloppy; her small breasts gained heft. She craved potato chips, white bread, expensive fruit. She was disgusted by vegetables and anything that came from a cow. The ultrasound revealed a looming skull, a knobby spine, a girl's budding genitals, a heart pulsing with barely a chest cavity to enclose it. There was an inscrutable creature inside her: was it angel or alien, darling or demon?

They'd gone around and around for a few months— a cycle of arguments and impasse—before Serena gave in. Any reasons she produced for why it would be better to remain childless couldn't best the claims Henry made. Her side was founded on negation, while he was angling for something, someone, a life. She couldn't win that one. It struck at the core of the fundamental clash between them—his native ebullience versus her inherent skepticism. But when she finally told him, *Okay, let's try,* it had to be as if she were doing it wholeheartedly. She had to act like him now.

At night in bed, his arms the rings around the Saturn of her enlarged belly, he lobbed names in her ear. "Olivia?"

"Too popular. It's number four for girls' names."

"You've done research?"

"It's common knowledge."

"Paige?"

"Cute. But too cute. Like, look, aren't we bookish."

Their daughter's name would chime through the house, through their days—the most corporeal of words. It had to be special but not too special—a name sturdy enough to last a lifetime.

"Too bad we weren't Soviets," Henry said, humming a Slavic-sounding tune. "Anna, Olga, Tatyana. Were they allowed anything else?"

"Svetlana."

"And Svetlana. That's why people miss Communism, I guess. Freedom from too much choice."

He kept trying till he got it right.

"Ella?"

"Still too popular—number twelve, I think."

"Willow?"

"Too naturey."

"Jade?"

"Too jewelryish."

"You're a pain in the ass. Belle. Bella. Beautiful beauty."

"No B names, remember? B.S. It fails the initial test."

Everything seemed wrong or already used up. Saturn lost its rings as Henry withdrew his arms and rolled away from her. "Okay," he grunted. "Eve."

Serena tested it out. "Eve Skolnik. Eve." Brief yet lingering. An exhale, an incantation: summer, twilight, rooftops. An evening, an eve. It was both a delicate sliver of time and an ordinary occasion.

"I like it," she said.

"Are you serious?"

"You suggested it."

"I was joking. Playing God."

"It's actually a good name. Plenty of people are named Adam and no one thinks about the association. It's not like Christian, or Jesús, or something."

The beeswax candle on the bureau cast the shadow of Henry's hand on the wall, a giant, animating shape. In the beginning was the name.

Eve was made of wailing, of banshee mouth and fighter fists. She might as well have been called There There, or What's The Matter, or Please Shut Up Already. Two states of being were known to her: fury and sleep.

The only person Serena had known who got this mad, this close to her, was her father. Like a shrill whistle blowing through her childhood, he yelled about shirkers and swindlers, lights left on when no one was home and all the Raisin Bran gone. His blue eyes sputtered in his red face; his outrage torpedoed out at his three domestic targets. Serena's mother yelled back sometimes, yelled at him to stop yelling. Her older brother developed a series of carefully modulated responses, tinged with irony subtle enough to fly beneath their dad's radar. Serena said nothing. She cowered at his cartoonish displays, but she was also impressed, in her shyness, that someone could release so much noise into the world. By the time she moved out of the house for college, she'd come to see how his own emotions were too much for him. She almost wished he'd go ahead and finish off one of his outbursts by hitting something or even someone, but he never did. He was a fly knocking wildly against the glass of the jar he was trapped in. When she was twenty-seven, a few months before she met Henry, her father died of a heart attack, and though he collapsed in the condo her parents had retired to, she pictured him in the living room of the house she'd grown up in, where she used to watch him as a kid, afraid he was yelling so hard he would burst open, and then she could feel sorry for him. She could gather up the pieces and fit them together, like one of those three-dimensional wooden puzzles, and place his heart back inside his chest, where it would stay safe.

The book about how to calm your baby said to swing her vigorously back and forth. Swing her harder than you'd think. Serena paced the living room, the dining room, the kitchen, with all the lights turned out, sailing Eve like a boat in a stormy sea. The edge of violence in it gave her more satisfaction than those tedious maternal tactics: cooing, nursing, humming lullabies. Sometimes she wondered how much vigor was too much, how much more force she would need to apply to be on the wrong side of those public service announcements on the bus: *Never shake your baby.*

Surely any day now, the child's real parents would return and collect her. Surely Serena and Henry were the surrogates, the starter parents. They'd done all right; they'd kept her alive. But soon they'd be relieved from their strange duties and change back into themselves. Time would resume its prevailing sensible arrangement: work by day, sleep straight through the darkest hours of night. They'd lie in bed embracing, two independent adult bodies, listening to each other's unremarkable breath.

Occasionally Henry, prone to nostalgia, would reminisce. *Remember when we had that baby?*

Yeah, that was crazy, Serena would say.

I miss her.

I know, but I bet she's doing great. I bet she's gone to a good home.

They took up the whole width of the sidewalk: Henry, Serena, and one stately stroller, on their way to the coffee shop. The stroller could rumble fleetly over snowdrifts and ice sheets; the handsome adjustable hood extended all the way down over the baby napping in the removable bassinet. It had been paid for by Henry's parents, who'd sent their granddaughter a bounty of expensive gifts and made no plans to book a flight and come meet her.

At twelve weeks old, Eve had been outside only a handful of times: the winter's fault, for packing the span of her life so far with bitter wind and piles of snow, and Eve's own fault for throwing a fit whenever she was placed in her posh stroller. Better to keep her inside where it was warm and the walls could contain her crying. But finally she seemed to be contemplating the idea that existence need not mean constant protest. She rode tranquilly this afternoon, staring up into the indigo fabric of the stroller hood as if, for all she knew, it was the sky.

This was the last day of Serena's maternity leave. Next week she'd resume her post at the library, in the hushed vault of books. She'd be called upon not for vital sustenance but to satisfy an intellectual curiosity. No one would scream or fall ill because she hadn't satisfied them. Since Eve's birth, Serena had been doing the bulk of the care while Henry raced to finish his projects. Now he would serve as the primary parent for the next three months until Eve started daycare. He would no doubt do a better job of it than Serena had—prove more patient and playful and loving.

At the coffee shop, they found a table where they could park the stroller, and ordered sickly sweet lattes in holiday flavors and a chocolate caramel brownie to share. They sat down facing each other, and Henry slid his hand across the table. "It's been a long time since we've done this."

"Yeah, before Eve. B.E.," Serena said, grasping his hand, and then they fell silent.

She remembered a time, shortly after they'd started

dating, when they sat at another coffee shop, holding hands without talking, the closeness of their bodies filling in for conversation (they'd made love just a few hours before, lingering in bed while their stomachs rumbled from hunger), until she started to worry that she wouldn't have enough to say to him every time they sat at a table together for the rest of their lives. She already wanted to marry him. But the upside of that probably not happening was that she wouldn't have to face all the times she couldn't think of anything to say, or ended up saying the wrong thing. If she estimated at least one meal a day together, nearly every week of the year, for fifty or so years—it was staggering.

A middle-aged woman with a to-go cup in her hand stopped in front of the stroller. Eve had woken up and was slithering her tongue in and out of her mouth. "What a calm, charming baby," the woman said.

"She's not calm," Serena said. "Don't let her fool you."

"But so adorable. How can you stand it?"

Eve smiled at the new face making gaga eyes at her.

"My two are all grown. The younger boy's a freshman in college this year, out in California, and the older one is off teaching English in Taiwan."

"Wonderful," Henry said. "Sounds like you did a great job."

Serena looked at the woman's meticulously arranged bright scarf, her scarlet lipstick and beaded earrings. How free she seemed, the accomplishment of her children's childhoods and adolescences behind her. She could be two decades older than Serena, but if she'd offered to trade places, at this moment Serena might have accepted.

"I'll tear myself away now," the woman said. "Congratulations." She walked out the door with a little wave.

"You're always trash-talking this kid," Henry said. "Wait till she's older. She'll get you back for that." They were no longer holding hands.

"I was being honest."

"Sweetheart, you could just take a compliment sometimes. Or take it on behalf of our daughter, anyway."

That's how the endearments came at her these days: tagged on to some implied insult. When he put his hand on her shoulder as they left the coffee shop, his touch was the steering, slightly patronizing grip of a father's.

How's her language?" the pediatrician asked at Eve's six-month visit.

"Her what?" Serena said, startled.

The doctor laughed. "I don't expect talking yet. I mean her vocalizations, babbling, that sort of thing. At this age it usually starts picking up and you'll want to encourage it. Talk to her as much as possible. Narrate your lives together."

As a kid Serena used to talk to herself a lot. At first she spoke aloud, and then later she silently mouthed her secret observations and her magic spells, her plays and her lists.

One day when she was ten, on a back-to-school shopping trip to the mall, her mother caught her moving her lips among the racks of pants and sweaters. "What are you doing?" she demanded. "Are you talking to someone?"

"No," Serena said. Obviously she wasn't talking to anyone; no one else was there.

"It looks strange," her mother said. "I'm telling you this for your own good, now that you're getting older. Keep your mouth closed, okay?"

And so Serena corrected it: shut her lips tight, redirected her words back up inside her head. It helped to picture them mounting a spiral staircase inside her skull, climbing up into her brain and disappearing there. It made her feel light-headed and empty, but she got used to it. And now, as an adult, the atmosphere of the library suited her well—everyone keeping their own counsel, people quietly approaching the reference desk only to have her send them back into the stacks. Returning to work after her maternity leave was the hushed relief she thought it would be.

But the rest of the time, when she was home, she was supposed to be communicating with an infant, chattering on when she had nothing to say and neither did the person she was speaking to. She read an article that said "motherese"—the high-pitched, exaggerated style people often used with babies—was good for their language development, helping them to distinguish where one word ended and the next one began. It was a matter of promoting her child's verbal abilities. So Serena attempted it sometimes, speaking stupid, obvious sentences to Eve:

I'm changing your diaper now. Let's turn up the heat. I'd better do laundry.

All boring stuff that hardly seemed worth mentioning. Perhaps the key was to say it with greater enthusiasm. *Can you believe we're out of milk? Telemarketers again?! Let's do our taxes, Eve. Let's do our taxes!* Serena was getting dumber, but Eve was learning. Sometimes, from her position on the floor, plastic keys clutched in one hand, squeaky bunny in the other, she would volley a string of earnest gibberish, as if unleashing some long-held conviction she had not, until this moment, found the opportunity to voice.

O n a Friday evening after work, Serena ground up brown rice in the blender and cooked it with water for ten minutes to fix a rice cereal more wholesome and probably better tasting than the commercial stuff you found at the grocery store, and then she mixed it with tahini and mashed banana to make a full nutritious meal. Eve was in daycare now, and Serena thought the women who worked there were great, certainly better than she was at taking care of a baby, and probably better than Henry too, who, for all his patience, and playfulness, and lovingness, wasn't very good about sticking to reliable routines. Still, she felt guilty that Eve had to leave home every day to be one of a group of babies competing for their caretakers' attention. Her guilt had led her to a book called *Super Baby Food* that encouraged parents (mothers, really) to make all their own homemade baby food, and

Serena, who had never much enjoyed making meals for anyone, found herself grudgingly concocting piles of mush. She put Eve in the high chair in the dining room, fastened a bib on, and started feeding her with a baby spoon: an exercise in frustration. Eve puckered her lips, allowing only the tiniest bit to seep into her mouth. And then Serena turned away because the kettle was boiling and she was dying for tea, and while her back was turned, Eve managed to grab gobs of cereal from the bowl, which apparently wasn't sufficiently out of reach, and she was smearing those gobs on herself and then throwing them down.

"Fuck!" Serena snatched the bowl away. "No, Eve, no!"

She was infuriated, all that preparation down the drain— not even down the drain, on the floor—and then Henry was saying, "How can you get mad at a baby?" He was just sitting there on the couch in the living room, watching her get on her hands and knees to sponge up the cereal.

"Why don't you help?" she screamed. "You wanted this. Not me. I never wanted to be a mother."

Henry pulled Eve out of the high chair and carried her into the kitchen. Serena kept her head down, scrubbing the floor hard. She'd said what couldn't be said, what she had promised herself she would never say. When she looked up again, Henry was washing the baby in the little tub that fit in the sink. He worked shampoo into the tufts of her hair, poured cupfuls of water over her head. Eve looked up, blinking, uncomplaining, into the stream. Usually when Henry bathed her he sang—nursery rhymes, Beatles songs, meandering tunes with goofy lyrics of his own invention.

You were born to sing to a baby was a sentence that often came into Serena's head when she watched him do this. She knew Henry would be pleased if she told him that, but she never had. She hadn't told him what a fantastic dad she thought he was.

He wasn't singing tonight. He turned on the radio to a news show, people calling in to air their political grievances.

Fuck, suck. She hadn't always been able to say those words. There was a time, in high school, when she'd tried to make herself say them, because everyone else did like it was no big deal, and it seemed to represent something to freely emit those so-called profanities: some coolness, some all-rightness with the world, in declaring with proper crudeness what was no good about it. Now it was laughable how easy such things were to say, how little they meant. Everything was about tone and context, shrugs and sighs: language as a kind of code with the key plain as day, a code cloaked not in mystery but in wry predictability. Even this mean thing she'd just said wasn't all that surprising.

She stayed up late reading an article that suggested having a child was the worst thing you could do to a relationship, that cited an alarming statistic for marriages that began flailing postpartum and never recovered. She read another article about how picky eating in early childhood might be a sign of incipient mental illness. She read a series of blog posts by a harried mother of three who called herself The Murderous Mommy, describing in detail all the things her kids did that made her want to kill them.

She read the comments posted by other women telling The Murderous Mommy what an awful person she was.

All day Saturday Serena and Henry skirted around each other, tending to their separate household tasks. It wasn't that different from the way they'd operated for years before Eve was born, when they chafed at each other's communication styles (or lack thereof) and couldn't find their way to talking things out. They would each become more self-righteously industrious—cleaning the kitchen, pulling weeds in the yard, rooting accumulated junk out of drawers. Now the baby just became part of that, both of them silently attentive to her, responding immediately to her needs as if making a show of competence, then withdrawing if the other person got there first. While Henry fed Eve an avocado, Serena grabbed a bin overflowing with papers and brought it upstairs to sort. Amid expired coupons, flyers announcing events already past, car repair receipts, clipped newspaper articles she hadn't read yet and probably never would— there was an envelope containing a piece of embossed paper with the state seal in one corner, the county court seal in another. CERTIFICATE OF LIVE BIRTH it said at the top, a reminder that it could have gone the other way. Then there was Eve's name, date and time of birth, the name of the hospital. There was a box for "Mother's Current Legal Name" and "Mother's Full Name Before First Married," and these were the same: Serena Marie Tanner. When she was a little girl, thinking about getting married one day, she imagined it as a kind of wedding gift her princely husband would give her: his last name in place of her father's, the ideal man becoming part of her official identity instead of the deeply flawed one. By the time she was a woman, even before her father died, she knew she wouldn't do that. She'd keep her original name for life, for better or worse, for what it represented: the family she came from, her refusal to follow a tradition that viewed a wife as her husband's property. And also because it need not represent anything at all; it was simply what she was accustomed to being called. She found an empty file folder and wrote Eve Tanner Skolnik on the tab, then folded up the birth certificate and placed it inside.

Sunday morning, when Eve woke Serena up late, past eight o'clock, Henry was already gone. He was probably out for a run, or treating himself to some kind of pleasure boost—a cinnamon raisin bagel from the deli, an affogato from the coffee shop, "a little sweetness in my life," he might say later, since Serena was bringing him down. She gave Eve a bottle, turned on some music—Lucinda Williams, loud—and then set the baby on the floor to scramble about. Soon Eve started screeching, what the pediatrician had called her pterodactyl screams. Had the pterodactyls been happy when they screamed like that? Eve seemed happy. She pulled herself up to stand against the couch and dipped her knees as if dancing to the music. If Henry were here, Serena would call him over to see, to watch it with her—their daughter's joy of life—hoping that might serve as a kind of truce.

When Eve needed a change, Serena carried her upstairs

for a new diaper and, for what it was worth, to change her out of pajamas and into clothes for the day. Henry's parents had sent an outfit that Eve would have no special occasion to wear before outgrowing it: a purple velvet dress with pearl buttons and ivory-colored tights. Why not put them on? Sunday best.

Serena held her up to the mirror, tilting their faces together. With Serena in the sweeping satin peignoir Henry had bought her for their anniversary, and Eve in her fancy attire, they might make some kind of portrait: Mother and Child in the Nursery. She'd never cared for Mary Cassatt, with those pastel domestic scenes—and yet if you and your child had been immortalized together in a painting, how could you help but be proud? Serena tested out a smile. A few months ago, Eve would have smiled automatically because Serena was smiling, but now she remained serious, the impulse to mimic replaced by watch and wait. Serena studied Eve's face in the mirror: dark eyes, wiggly eyebrows, bumpy chin. There were bits of her you could half match with each of her parents' features, but really Eve looked like herself, like her own indignant person. Serena kissed her cheek. "Oh love bug," she said. Lately, when the two of them were alone in the house, these pet names had begun to ooze out of her, goofy word combinations she'd never uttered before in her life. *Sweetie dear. Pumpkin pie. Sugar bean.*

Where did they come from? Biology meeting language: instinctive affection arousing linguistic silliness. Months of sleep deprivation, diminishing brain cells, and baby-board-book speak. The kid was driving her crazy: plunging her into madness and frustration and a primordial syrupy love. She'd never experienced such wild fluctuations—in the baby, which was natural for a baby, she supposed, but in herself too.

"Evie, devie?" Serena kissed her again and again. "You're my bunny cupcake. My little buffalo bird. My chummy chum."

Suddenly Henry was there, just behind them, framed in the mirror. With the music still blasting, Serena hadn't heard him open the front door and walk up the stairs. He wore that look of amusement, both ironic and tender, that she thought of as distinctly his: a look that could shift the molecules in the air, change everything for the moment.

"Let's hear that again," he said.

Parental Fade

You can do it the long and painful way or the quick and painful way, the pediatrician says. The quick and painful way— otherwise known as crying it out—means putting the baby in her crib at bedtime, shutting the door, leaving her there till morning. Whatever it takes to ignore the cries—blast the TV, have noisy sex, take turns leaving the house—this is what we must do.

The long and painful way is called a parental fade. Put the baby in her crib and get comfortable in the rocking chair. Don't pick the baby up. Try not to even touch her. Wait for her to settle her own self down, cry herself to sleep. Each night, move the rocker farther away from the crib. Remain in the room for a shorter amount of time. Crying it out takes a few nights at most. Parental fade may take several weeks.

Either way works. It's up to you, the pediatrician says. He is the gentlest, smilingest man we have ever met. He sings our baby's name when we bring her in to his office. He keeps a musical frog on the ceiling, sets it swinging as he draws the needle for her shots. *Look at the frog,* he croons happily.

We cringe. We fear the baby will develop a phobia of frogs. We're exhausted, despairing, mad at each other and at all parenting manuals, at all parents whose babies don't regard their cribs as horrible cages of doom. Our insurance covers a thirty-minute sleep consultation; it's coded as a necessary medical intervention. Now our thirty minutes are up. The pediatrician offers a final compassionate smile. *Believe me, it works. You'll be surprised. You'll be relieved. You'll be okay.*

In the car on the way home, we consider our options. Can we get a hotel room for the weekend, pay the babysitter to do this cry-it-out-all-night thing? Can we commit to two weeks of being stationed in a rocking chair, pretending to ignore our screaming child? Can we accept that a baby crying is nothing more than a baby crying—that this is only the first of many battles, and we must be strong, we must not yield, we must stay fixed on the goal for the good of all?

Our daughter, in her rear-facing car seat, gnaws on the legs of a rubber giraffe. She is ten months old: crawling, pulling herself up to stand, pointing, clapping, shaking her head no, saying "da" and "ma," though not necessarily in reference to us. She has two teeth on top and one about to break through on the bottom; she eats mashed sweet potato and peas and banana, but not spinach or apricots or squash. She has her father's broad forehead and rounded nose, her mother's hazel eyes and loosely curling brown hair. She will fall asleep in the stroller and the car seat, in our bed and in our arms. When she's asleep in our bed, she sprawls out, hits and kicks us, sends one of us to the couch. The other one sleeps fitfully, afraid she might suffocate or roll off the unattended side. If we sneak her into the crib, she usually wakes up. If the sneaking thing actually works, we tiptoe around and speak in hushed voices. Perversely, we miss her.

We are in our forties; we look it and feel it. This doesn't fit with our vision of how the world should work. We should be twenty-three always, uncertain of the future yet convinced of the promise it holds. Though we could potentially be the parents of a twenty-three-year-old, we feel too young for parenthood. Mama and Dada? How can these words apply to us? We still have trouble with Ma'am and Sir.

No, we have to remind ourselves: this is how the world works. Our own parents and stepparents are senior citizens: retired, ailing, acquiring new knees and hips, losing their memories. All of our grandparents are gone. Pictures of these people from another time line our mantel. They are young there: dashing in their military uniforms, zaftig in their bathing costumes, stern in their wedding attire. We would like to have known them then, but we were born too late. The '70s will be as remote to our daughter as the '30s are to us.

So, it's decided, starting tonight. Parental fade. An aging rock band, a haircut for the going bald, a chronic illness, the way of the world. We wish we could do quick and painful, but let's be realistic. As soon as we put the baby in her crib, she'll stand up and scream. She'll either never lie back down or she'll collapse in a mangled heap. She'll cry so hard she'll throw up and then choke on her own vomit. We'll have to go in and check on her, and all will be lost.

Actually, we believe the pediatrician is right. The baby would be fine, she'd work it out on her own. In the morning, when we entered her bedroom, guilt-ridden and spent, our daughter would smile her smile of delight— her oldest and best trick—the smile she offers to anyone who shows her a bit of interest, but most of all to her parents, who are most in need of it. She's a narcissistic insomniac, preventing others from sleeping if she cannot. A sentimental whore, refusing to sleep alone in her own bed. The most grating of alarm clocks: no radio option, no snooze button. But here are her trump cards: she smiles as if she herself had discovered joy, and she never holds a grudge.

We just can't do quick and painful, though we're not those kind of parents—the ones who declare on their blogs that letting your baby cry herself to sleep leaves psychological scars, gives the kid lifelong feelings of insecurity and abandonment. Our objection is not on philosophical grounds, nor is it out of genuine fear for the baby's well-being. (We believe fundamentally—we have to believe—that the baby will always be all right.) No, we're softies, weaklings, cowards. It's easier for us to do things the hard way.

Instead of the typical Saturday frenzy—going to the grocery store, cleaning, vacuuming, doing laundry, making calls, sorting through mail, shopping online for time-and-space-saving devices, clipping our toenails, while the baby is shuttled from her stroller, to her jumper, to the rug, to a parent who keeps one hand free for other tasks—we spend the afternoon, both of us together, playing with the baby. We lie down on the floor and let her take it from there. She climbs on top of us, examines our belly buttons, our teeth, our ears. She gets closer to our faces than anyone would dare. She peers into our eyes with an expression of both pleasure and astonishment, as if to say: Now that I have you, what will I do with you? She grabs wooden rings, rubber ducks, tennis balls. She taps on the plastic protectors we've installed in the electrical outlets. Everything is toy and teether, everything should be graspable, everything must be mouthed. She flaps her arms when we bring out the canister of Cheerios. When we tell her not to play with the fireplace grate, she stops and starts, stops and starts. She makes a goofy face: half pig, half rabbit. She comes galumphing across the room to smash a tower of blocks with her fist. She prefers the monkey to the teddy bear, *Go, Dog. Go!* to *Goodnight Moon,* crawling to cuddling. One day she'll speak in sentences, make up stories, reason her way through problems, feel things she will choose to talk about or not.

But for now, she knows only that she wants us. And we're tired. As we stack plastic cups and wind the mechanical mouse, we debate which one of us will work the shift tonight, set the parental fade into motion. One of us rocked her to sleep for two hours last night. One of us got up with her at 5:45 this morning. One of us has a slightly higher tolerance for tears. One of us is a more comforting presence. One of us has more work to do tomorrow. One of us gave birth to her, nursed her for eight months.

One of us will do it, never mind which one. The off-duty parent can hear the wailing anyway, the banging on the crib, the coaxing sounds, the uselessly cheerful songs. The waiting-outside parent knows—from the interlude of silence, followed by renewed fuming—that the inside-the-room parent has cheated: picked the baby up for a moment and then put her back down. There's the pull to give in, to give up. But we told the doctor we'd try this. We joked about it to our friends. We promised each other and we promised ourselves. We're trying to remember what life was like before this baby. Interesting, mundane. Hopeful, fearful. Easy, tiring. Good, disappointing. In many ways the same as it is now. People say that a baby changes everything, but is that true? Are we more patient or less? More generous or more selfish? More engaged with the world or more in retreat from it? More accepting of mortality or more frightened of dying? These are things to think about, lying in bed with a pitiful soundtrack or rocking and rocking in a sad, dark room.

The baby is still crying but she's losing steam. The hiccups are setting in; the defeated, catching-the-breath sobs. In a way, those fading whimpers are harder to hear than the howls. Babies in terrible circumstances, we've read—starving babies, orphaned babies, babies living through wars—eventually stop crying all the time when they realize that crying will do nothing. The learned silence of a suffering baby: worse than all the yelling a healthy, privileged baby can muster.

It's been quiet for some time. The door to the baby's room opens and clicks shut. The emotionally exhausted parent enters the bedroom to report to the other one. We're two adult bodies alone in bed tonight. We spoon in our clothes, keep our hands still. Sex is a sport for childless couples and retirees. Sex is a dream we used to have together. That's partly why we're doing this—to take back the bedroom, to unroll a condom at midnight (we're not taking any chances) instead of a bottle liner that resembles a condom. Once it was romantic to trade sleep for sex. Now it's just dumb. When the baby wakes up again three hours later, the second-shift parent assumes the position, watches the subject through the bars, a primatologist monitoring a screaming chimp.

Let's be scientists, then, attentive but detached, asking questions, recording observations, setting emotional impulses aside. The baby is crying. Why do babies cry?

A primal reaction, an evolutionary advantage. Long ago there was a race of tranquil, noncrying babies. When they wanted milk, when they wanted comfort, when they wanted to be picked up and rocked to sleep, their faces simply assumed sweet and hopeful expressions. A small number of parents always responded to these cues, kept their sweet and hopeful babies safe, taught them to speak, to make polite requests, to shrug in a *that's life* way when they didn't get the things they wanted. But the majority of parents didn't do so well, being blessed with an undemanding, mum's-the-word baby. Their babies were malnourished, caught colds and then pneumonia, got lost in the woods, trapped in caves, eaten by animals. Eventually this race of babies died out. The shriekers, the protesters, the *you-better-fucking-do-something* babies— these were the ones that survived to pass on their talent for bellowing, for making themselves heard with a sound that reverberated inside their parents' bodies, in that place between the stomach and the rib cage, the seat of love and panic.

Babies like this baby here, a fine exemplum of the species. This baby, refusing to accept that her caretaker is right there within view, and yet offers no warmth, no breath, no scent, no back-and-forth cradling in the arms: the seat of reassurance and surrender.

Tonight, study the room, a room we considered carefully before the baby arrived, choosing what color to paint the walls (the delicate gray of pigeons' wings, of the sky before snow); arranging the furniture (Ikea, Craigslist); putting up pictures (Matisse dancers, Chagall village, a monkey at a typewriter painted by a friend's kid). This room isn't as nice as the rooms of other babies we know: the one whose parents made the furniture themselves, the one whose parents are professional designers, the one whose parents are rich. But we like to think it's tasteful and comforting. We like to think that the baby, though she seems to prefer every other room in the house to this one, will come to think of it as her own special space.

Tonight, the light is dimmed to the lowest setting the dimmer switch will allow, obscuring the features of the baby's tearstained face, while affording an eventual smooth exit from the room. The light fixture resembles a breast: the suspended globe, the pointy nub. In the almost dark, the pieces of furniture look like congenial beasts. The baby's howling is the voice of the jungle, its animating force. Each creature within has staked out its territory. Here is the bureau: a bulwark, a hoarder. Keeper of clothes previously worn by other fast-growing babies: a series of multicolored, spotted, striped, and flowered things that fit for now. The bottom drawer holds the next size up, clothing for a giant, until it's outgrown and becomes impossibly small. Here is the changing table, warden of excrement, of domestication, of civilized waste disposal, of keeping one's bottom covered and dry. Here is the bookshelf, cleared of half its books, the ones in danger of being torn apart, stripped from their spines. The sturdy, simple ones remain, full of rabbits and moons, cats and colors, successful bedtimes and journeys by boat. Here is the mobile: a peaceable kingdom, an airborne zoo. The elephant is pink, the parrot stands as tall as the giraffe, the tortoise keeps pace with the cheetah. All look friendly, all dance at the prompting of a parent's hand. And here is the baby, lord over all. Beware her wild cries! Beware her human ferocity!

We'd rather not think of ourselves as a *we*. We never wanted to be like those couples—all *we think this* and *we like that*. We don't share one body, one mind, one heart. We discussed this before we got married, before we cosigned the loan on the house, before we united that egg with that sperm, before we joined our last names with a hyphen (which has to stop somewhere—if a hyphenated daughter marries a hyphenated son, how many hyphens can their children bear?). We're still two people, taking turns feeling depressed and contented, giving and receiving hugs, saying *I'm sorry* and *It's okay*. Two people negotiating over who will call the plumber; who will change the diaper; who will get out of the house first in the morning; who will be right; who will win by shouting, by silence, by kindness. Two people angling for the newspaper, for the last piece of cake, for more time for ourselves, for more sympathy for our grievances, for the right to remain in bed while the other one stumbles out of it and into the room next door.

When you are older, which one of us will you confide in? Which one of us will you begrudgingly admire? To which one of us will you assign the most blame? Now we can joke and curse, mutter and huff in front of you all day while you go about your baby business, finding everything within reach: bottle, toys, teething ring, parents. Now, in the room next to yours, we can make love—again, at last—and you won't even wonder at our strange pleasure sounds. How long do we have before you begin to track the flash in the eyes, the set of a jaw? How long before the word *parents* carries with it a sense of duty and burden, irritation and embarrassment? When you are old enough to consider such questions, will you believe—your existence aside— that we made the right choice in choosing each other? Will you keep our wedding picture on your mantel, missing the people you never knew?

Think of things that fade. Jeans and hair dye. Paper and summer. Music, clapping, laughter. The sex drive. The glow of human skin. Think of things that don't fade. The colors in paintings by the Old Masters. Evolutionary principles. A certain order of things—earth orbiting sun, spring following winter, children succeeding parents.

We remember nights when we couldn't sleep as kids. The house was quiet, the tree outside the bedroom window loaded down with blossoms or skeletal in the dark. At first we celebrated our freedom: crept downstairs and pulled *The Joy of Sex* from its camouflaged place on the bookshelf; ravaged the Häagen-Dazs; turned on a late-night movie about a bulimic or a serial killer; opened the drawer with our parents' private papers, thought better of it, then closed the drawer and went back to bed. Sheep leapt across a meadow, counting anxieties; the sandman got into a motorcycle accident on the highway. We tried everything: lying on a beach and letting the waves wash over us, relaxing every part of our bodies, masturbating against pillows and dolls, petitioning gods we were supposed to believe in. We envisioned catching fly balls, living out in the woods, punching some people in the face and kissing others on the lips. We imagined that our parents were not our parents, that our real parents were out there somewhere: movie star princess and sorcerer king, Judy Blume and Cal Ripken, Jr., perfectly normal mom and perfectly normal dad.

Someday we will tell you this story. How helpless we felt, how weak, how unprepared, how we couldn't imagine you falling asleep on your own—and for years you've been doing it: lying down in your bed in the dark and trusting that soon the darkness will overtake you. It will please you to hear this, the way it's pleasing to think of oneself as a baby: tiny, goofy, not quite yourself. To think of your parents younger, uninitiated, baffled by parenthood, people in their own right. People like you and not like you at all. Someday, if everything goes according to plan, we will die before you.

Now here we are, in the chair by your crib, inching farther away each night as your crying fades, as you come to rely on your miniature pillow, your transitional object, your adaptable brain, your inner resources, everything you have that isn't us. We don't believe that babies are little angels. We don't believe that God sent you to us. Before you were born, we were babies ourselves, then children, teenagers, adults with no dependents. We had two mothers, two fathers, three stepparents. We loved other people, left them and lost them. We had abortions and miscarriages.

Somehow, we thought, we will become parents, but the child that would grant us this title was no one we had ever seen before in our lives. Before, it could have been anyone. Now it can only be you.

ACKNOWLEDGMENTS

The following good people have been instrumental to the making of this book during its many years of gestation.

First, I'm indebted to my agent Renée Zuckerbrot, who is attentive, meticulous, thoughtful, and funny, and whose belief in story collections carried me through.

Margo Shickmanter is a dream of an editor. A million thanks to her for her challenges and cheerleading, and to everyone behind the scenes at Doubleday.

I'm ever grateful for my inspiring and empathetic friends. Particular thanks to those whose conversation about matters related to these stories informed my thinking and bolstered my spirits: Nicola Hesketh, Sara Despres, Debra Shushan, Sarna Lapine, Elyssa Kline, Rachel Sussman, Angela Kase, Lysa Rivera, Mineko Akishige, Roxanne Spiegel, Maya Barzilai, Emily Goedde, Ellie Abrons, Zeynep Gürsel, and Ami Walsh.

Without the generosity and kindness of Erica Frantz and Cliff Williams, I'd be an even more hassled mother than I am. *Muchísimas gracias* to them, and to all the teachers and babysitters whose wise and loving care has enriched my children's lives and allowed me the time to work.

My writing group in Ann Arbor offered suggestions on a number of these stories and kept me on task and in good company. Thanks to Lori Eaton, Ann Epstein, Amy Gustine, Marni Hochman, Keith Hood, Danielle LaVaque-Manty, Paul Many, Cathy Mellett, and Sonja Srinivasan.

I'm also grateful to Jonathan Dee; the University of Arizona Poetry Center; and Christine Hume at Eastern Michigan University, who brought me on to teach creative writing.

My parents, Leslie and Ira Rosenwaike, have given me a lifetime of support and encouragement. I wish my grandmothers, Gertrude Felberbaum and Zillah Levine, were still here to be properly thanked.

In both the literary and the parenting realms, I depend on and admire Cody Walker beyond measure. Thank you for being a brilliant editor, an amazing dad, and my best friend.

And finally, love and treats to my daughters Zia and Ani, whose spirited take on the world makes me truly happy.